William Norris

Mr. Chaine's sons

A Novel. Vol. 2

William Norris

Mr. Chaine's sons
A Novel. Vol. 2

ISBN/EAN: 9783337273743

Printed in Europe, USA, Canada, Australia, Japan

Cover: Foto ©Andreas Hilbeck / pixelio.de

More available books at **www.hansebooks.com**

MR. CHAINE'S SONS

MR. CHAINE'S SONS

A Novel

BY

W. E. NORRIS

AUTHOR OF 'THIRLBY HALL,' 'A BACHELOR'S BLUNDER,'
'THE ROGUE,' ETC.

IN THREE VOLUMES

VOLUME II.

LONDON

RICHARD BENTLEY & SON, NEW BURLINGTON ST.

Publishers in Ordinary to Her Majesty the Queen

1891

CONTENTS

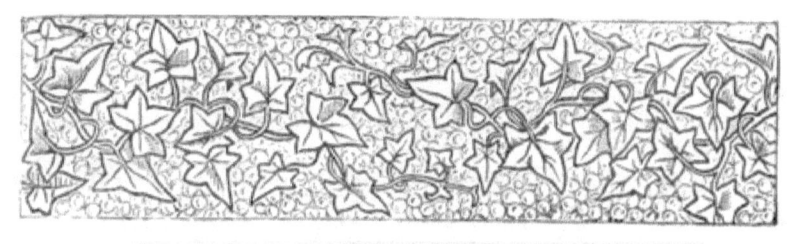

MR. CHAINE'S SONS

CHAPTER XVII

JUSTICE AND EXPEDIENCY

By noontide on the following day St. Albyn's
and its neighbourhood were in the full enjoyment of a piece of news which for interest
and excitement fairly eclipsed anything that
had been known to occur in that part of the
world within living memory.   Murders, of
course, there had been from time to time,
in consonance with the law of averages;
but these had for the most part been of a
vulgar and commonplace kind, unattended by
any mystery and worthy of remark only in
so far as they had served to prove the lamentable depravity of the lower classes.   The

extraordinary and unaccountable crime which had been perpetrated upon the confines of Mr. Chaine's property was a very different thing from the brutal assault of a detected poacher or the savagery of a drunken artisan, and the more one inquired into the affair the more strange did it appear. The ascertained facts were that, early that morning, Mr. Fraser had been found lying dead in a wood not many yards distant from the highway, that the body exhibited unmistakable marks of violence, and that, as the deceased had not been despoiled of his watch or his money, the hypothesis of robbery must be excluded. There was also a somewhat sinister rumour abroad to the effect that he had last been seen in company with Mr. John Chaine, at whose house he was said to have dined and spent the evening. This, to be sure, was not in itself an incriminating circumstance; still it was generally felt amongst the old gentlemen and old ladies who discussed the affair that John Chaine would have to give some account of the manner in which he had parted from his guest. Because, although it might sound rather ill-natured to say so, everybody was aware that relations had latterly been somewhat strained between John Chaine and the violinist.

It was not until after midday that her servants communicated the tragic intelligence to Ida, who was as much horrified as she was distressed by it. She had been in a manner fond of the dead man: he had seemed to understand her, and had been kind to her, and, despite certain little affectations which she had disliked, she had found him more in sympathy with her ideas and easier to talk to than any other neighbour of hers; so that her first emotion was that very natural one of purely selfish sorrow with which most of us have sad reason to be acquainted. After a time she began to wonder, as other people were wondering, what enemy so harmless a mortal could have contrived to earn for himself; but even then it never crossed her mind to suspect her husband, who indeed, by Wilfrid's account, had been in no state to leave the house at the hour when the murder must have been committed. She had gathered that there had been an altercation between John and Fraser, and this she had not regretted, because it had seemed to her that an open quarrel was more desirable than an armed truce ; nor had she had at all regretted John's departure for London, feeling that it would be to her advantage that he should have a day in which to reflect over and repent of his misconduct. But in the presence of this terrible catastrophe her irritation against her husband died away. He would, she felt sure, be both shocked and grieved on learning how the man whom he had so ridiculously imagined to be his rival had been removed from his path ; and, now that poor Fraser was dead and gone, she might, without any great sacrifice of self-respect, condescend to explanations which she would not have cared to give during his lifetime. At the bottom of her heart she was aware that she had married one who, though not pleasant to live with,

had nevertheless the instincts of a gentleman.

She was therefore wholly unprepared for
what lay before her when, soon after luncheon,
she was informed that old Mr. Chaine was
in the drawing-room and wished to see her.
That the object of her father-in-law's visit
was to request some particulars as to what
had occurred at her house on the previous
evening she, of course, guessed; but she was
a good deal surprised to find the old man in
such a state of agitation that his first words
were scarcely intelligible. He was trembling
from head to foot; he seemed to breathe with
difficulty; and as he stood beside her, holding
her hand, his face had an expression of pity,
and almost of remorse, which she was quite
unable to account for.

She made him sit down and rang for a
glass of water, saying, 'You must have walked
here too fast; I dare say you have been
upset, too, by this dreadful news about Mr.
Fraser. You want to know whether I can
throw any more light upon the mystery,

isn't that it? Well, I am afraid I can't. I
didn't see Mr. Fraser after dinner, and all
I know is that he went away about eleven
o'clock. Wilfrid can tell you more than
I can.'

She was obliged to put the questions which
she saw in Mr. Chaine's face for him, for he
seemed to be incapable of uttering them himself. But presently he made an effort and
regained something of his accustomed self-
command.

'My dear,' said he, in that deep voice
which had once roused the echoes of St.
Stephen's, and which was now so broken
and uncertain, 'Wilfrid will tell me nothing.
He is right, perhaps; I don't blame him;
probably I should act as he is acting if I
were in his place. But the suspense is more
than I can bear. All I implore of you is to
reassure me if you can. If you say that
that is impossible, I shall understand, and
I will promise to ask nothing more.'

The colour faded out of Ida's cheeks,
leaving her as white as a sheet. For a

moment she was terrified; but soon her common sense came to her aid, and she perceived at once how natural the old man's apprehensions were and how little ground there was for them.

'How you frightened me!' she exclaimed involuntarily. 'Fortunately, I can tell you now what I should not have liked to tell you if it had not been to relieve your mind of a much worse idea. The truth is that John drank more wine than he ought to have done last night, and I am afraid he must have been quite intoxicated when Mr. Fraser left. I was very much vexed when I heard about it; but now I am most thankful, for I see what an awful accusation he may be preserved from by it. You have evidently misunderstood Wilfrid. Naturally, he did not wish to betray his brother, and I suppose, knowing what the facts were, it never struck him that you might suspect John of having been the murderer.'

Mr. Chaine shook his head, which had fallen forward upon his breast. 'My poor child,' said

he, 'you only confirm my fears. Wilfrid
has confessed to me what he apparently did
not think it wise to tell you, that your
husband and Mr. Fraser came to blows last
night and that the affray ended by John's
knocking the other man down by a blow on
the head with a heavy stick. Wilfrid, it is
true, asserts that his brother was under the
influence of liquor and also professes his firm
conviction that the blow was not sufficient
to cause death; but I can elicit nothing
further from him, and I am persuaded that
he is keeping something back. Do I understand that you did not see John last night
or before he started this morning?'

Ida made a gesture of assent. 'The last
time that I saw John,' she answered, 'was
when I left the dining-room after dinner.
I thought—I supposed that he was ashamed
of himself and did not want to be brought
face to face with me.'

She had turned sick and faint all of a
sudden, and the four walls seemed to be
revolving round her.

'Did he leave any message?' pursued Mr. Chaine. 'Do you expect him back to-night?'

At that moment a telegram was brought to her, which she perused without remark, conscious of the eager scrutiny of the butler, who took a very long time in getting as far as the door. But as soon as the man was out of the room, she handed the slip of paper to Mr. Chaine and fell back in her chair, pressing her fingers tightly together.

The words which met the unhappy father's eyes deprived him at once of all doubt and all hope. 'Detained here on business,' was John's curt announcement. 'Cannot fix date for return yet.'

'You see how it is,' Mr. Chaine said sadly, as he gave back the telegram. 'John does not mean to return, and all you and I can do now, Ida, is to pray that he never may. The hand of God has fallen heavily upon me in my old age; but your case is harder than mine. I will not attempt to console you, nor is it in my power to make any reparation to you; but what little I can do I will, and so far as mere money is concerned, you may rest assured that you will continue to be treated in all respects as if you were my own daughter. John will henceforth be dead to me: I presume that he is aware of that, and that he will make his arrangements accordingly. A man may, in a fit of passion, hastily and unintentionally kill another—such things have occurred before now in the history of our family, I am sorry to say — but I believe this is the first time that any one bearing the name of Chaine has been known to seek safety by flight.'

'He may come back,' murmured Ida; 'he may not have known what he had done. I will telegraph to him at once.'

'Do you know where he is?' asked Mr. Chaine. 'He gives no address, you see. No, my dear, we must face facts and bear them as bravely as we can. If he had been brave enough to face a coroner's jury, he might very probably have been acquitted; but I fear that his conscience accused him—I fear that this was no unpremeditated crime. As I said before, we can only pray now that he may succeed in effecting his escape.'

That was certainly what Ida felt most inclined to pray for. It was hardly to be expected of her that she should take a more merciful view of her husband's behaviour than his own father had been able to adopt; latterly she had been very near hating John, and she had always despised him; after this, she could not possibly desire to be bound to so cowardly a criminal by any closer tie than that which must unite her to him as long as he lived. After the old man had crept away, bending under the burden of his disgrace, she sat for more than an hour, with her hands idly clasped in her lap, wondering what she had done to deserve the affliction that had fallen upon her. Perhaps, if she had loved her husband or believed in him, she might have made some effort, however futile, to seek him out; but it never occurred to her to do that. Like Mr. Chaine, she was persuaded, not only of his guilt, but that he had sinned deliberately. Wilfrid, she assumed, would make out as good a case for him as could be made ; possibly he might not be pronounced a wilful murderer ; still she perceived that he was self-condemned by the mere fact of having run away, and, whatever might be his fate, her own was irrevocably decided. She may be pardoned for thinking of herself, since her husband had apparently taken so little thought for her, and perhaps some kindly-disposed persons may even be found to sympathise with her heart-broken cry of, 'Oh, Arthur, this is my punishment for having doubted you ! If only I had had a little more faith and a little more courage I shouldn't have been left now with nothing but a ruined life to look forward to !'

It is customary to sneer at coroner's inquests, which in truth have done something to earn the obloquy so freely bestowed upon them ; but there are occasions on which neither the ingenuity of the coroner nor that of his jury can avail to bring about a miscarriage of justice, and the inquiry which was duly held upon the body of the late owner of Hatton Park was conducted in harmony with

what appeared to be the dictates of common-
sense. Wilfrid, of course, was the only important witness, and his evidence was not the
less telling because it was given with evident
reluctance. He admitted having seen his
brother fell Mr. Fraser by a blow with his
walking-stick, but seemed to be somewhat
confused when reminded that, according to
the medical testimony, death had resulted not
from that blow but from suffocation. When
pressed to say whether there had been any
subsequent struggle, he declared himself unable
to answer negatively or affirmatively upon his
oath. To the best of his belief, the affray had
ended with the blow described; but he would
not swear that it had. His chief anxiety had
been to drag away his brother, who, as he had
already mentioned, was not quite sober at the
time, and he could only affirm that it had
never entered into his head to dread any fatal
consequences from what had taken place.

This was naturally regarded as very
damaging testimony. Every allowance was
made for the cruel position in which poor Mr.

Wilfrid Chaine was placed ; still it was as impossible to attach implicit credence to his statements as it was to doubt that his brother had fled the country. The evidence of Clark, the butler, was likewise most unsatisfactory. From this unwilling witness it was elicited that his master had been in a state of more or less complete inebriety on the night of the fatal event ; that he had left for London early on the following morning, leaving no address and taking no luggage, except a hand-bag, with him ; that he had been expected to return the same day, but had not returned ; and that nothing had been heard of him since, beyond a telegram to Mrs. Chaine, in which he had stated that he was detained in town. Ida herself, who was very mercifully dealt with, could only confirm these assertions. The inevitable result was a verdict of manslaughter against John Chaine and the issue of a warrant for the apprehension of the fugitive.

To Ida and to old Mr. Chaine such a result was terrible enough ; but to Wilfrid it was not quite sufficiently terrible to be reassuring. A verdict of wilful murder would have been a good deal more to the purpose. It was very possible, and not so very unlikely, that John, upon more mature reflection, might decide to risk the pains and penalties attaching to the crime of manslaughter—of which crime, indeed, he had not yet been proved guilty. Moreover, if he read the newspapers, he could not but perceive that it was not he who had killed Leonard Fraser. True, he might have considerable difficulty in establishing the fact of his innocence ; but that was just what a stupid fellow like John would be sure not to realise.

' I ought to have told him to bolt off to the Continent at once,' mused Wilfrid regretfully ; ' in my unfortunate anxiety to help him to baffle the police, I quite forgot those accursed daily papers. Well, one comfort is that, if he does come back, he will be obliged to admit that I did the best I could for him, and another comfort is that he will never be forgiven by the governor. As for his story about Jessie, that will hardly hold water now, I should think.'

But as the days passed on, it became in-

creasingly evident that neither Wilfrid's apprehensions nor those of his father and his sister-
in-law were to be verified. It was, of course,
a time of the deepest anxiety, sorrow and
humiliation for the Chaine family; a time
which one of them, at least, hardly expected
or wished to survive; a time when, as he
could not but be aware, all England was
talking about him and all his old friends
pitying him with that kind of pity which is
almost worse than condemnation. Yet there
was just one spark of consolation in the fact
that John remained untraced and untraceable.
It was at once found out that he had spent a
few hours at a hotel and that he had drawn
£300 from the bank; but beyond that nothing
was discovered, and although the police were,
as usual, stated to be in possession of a clue,
their efforts had no result. To outwit the
English police is said to be a task of no super-
human difficulty; at all events, some rather
dull-witted criminals have managed to accomplish it, and it seemed that the name of
John Chaine would now have to be added to

that successful list.   The risk of his capture must, it was true, always remain as a menace to the tranquillity of those who would so thankfully have received news of his death ; but that peril diminished every day, and at length Ida began to feel as if it might be possible for her, some time in the dim future, to hold up her head once more.

Meanwhile, old Mr. Chaine, who had no such hope for himself, hastened to square accounts with a world which he only longed to leave, and performed an act of justice and expediency by appointing his second son as the heir to his estates.

CHAPTER XVIII

VIOLET VISITS THE AFFLICTED

No one disputes the truth of that threadbare maxim of La Rochefoucauld's to the effect that the misfortunes of our best friends are not altogether displeasing to us; but any one who would kindly explain why that strange and discreditable fact should be a fact would confer a boon upon the human race by making an appreciable addition to the common knowledge of our common nature. It can hardly be accounted for by the assertion that breaks. whether tragic or otherwise, in the monotony of daily existence must needs be welcome; yet, in default of a more plausible suggestion, that may be accepted for what it is worth, and doubtless a superabundance of leisure, together with the possession of a comfortable and assured income, are apt to exercise a somewhat deteriorating influence upon us all.

The worthy Canons of St. Albyn's, with their worthy wives, really liked Mr. Chaine and Lady Elizabeth, while they could not be said to dislike Ida; they were sincerely sorry for these poor people in their terrible affliction and they quite thought that the sudden death of so young a man as Leonard Fraser was a most appalling incident. Nevertheless, since the inscrutable wisdom of Providence had decreed that this visitation should occur, they found an immensity of satisfaction in talking it over, and it may be surmised that the evasion of the presumed culprit was a secret disappointment to some of them.

'One can't help feeling that it is so shockingly cowardly of him,' Mrs. Pickersgill said. 'Of course he may have had reasons and excuses for being exasperated—that is perfectly possible—but that a man who has been betrayed into committing such an awful sin should not have the courage to face the consequences is, I confess, almost as bad, to my mind, as the sin itself.'

Canon Pickersgill slightly disturbed the serene height of the general sense of morality by remarking that, if he had had the bad luck to slay a fellow-creature unintentionally, he should without doubt have taken to his heels and never ceased running until he was stopped by a policeman ; but Canon Pickersgill was notoriously addicted to misplaced levity. He could only wag his head and draw down the corners of his mouth when he was reminded that the worst feature in this lamentable affair was the strong suspicion of its having been premeditated.

Of course no such suggestion, nor any allusion to the painful topic, could be ventured upon in the presence of the Dean, who described himself as 'stricken down,' and who, in truth, was very unhappy until it transpired that his daughter's pecuniary position would not be altered for the worse by the unmerited calamity which had fallen upon her. His piety was sincere, so far as it went ; he recog-

nised the hand of God in all things ; and when
he had ascertained that old Mr. Chaine had
been kindness itself to Ida, begging her not
to dream of quitting the White House, and
promising to make ample testamentary provision for her, he did not omit to return
thanks in the proper quarter at the proper
time. He even went so far as to say to
himself that the removal of Leonard Fraser,
notwithstanding the tragic fashion of its
accomplishment, might prove a blessing in
disguise to an anxious father, and he preached
a sermon in the cathedral upon the duty of
submission to the Divine will which earned
the admiration of all who were privileged to
listen to it.

So, by degrees, excitement and curiosity
died down, as they always do. John Chaine,
it was evident, had contrived to cheat the
gallows ; nothing further was likely to be
learnt as to the motives of his crime ; a distant
relative of the late Leonard Fraser was discovered, and the interest of St. Albyn's became
transferred to this new owner of Hatton Park,

who was a widower with a large family and who was not so advanced in life as to exclude the probability of his marrying a second time.

'Another chance for an eligible young spinster,' remarked Violet Stanton to her mother, one morning. 'I suppose you will make haste to call upon the last edition of the Fraser family.'

'I shall do nothing of the sort,' answered her mother in a vexed tone; 'I shall wait until we meet them, and I shall not call then unless I am clearly given to understand that they wish it. No one, I am sure, can accuse me of being pushing. As you know, I haven't even been to Chaine Court since this dreadful business, though I should have liked to let Lady Elizabeth know how truly I sympathise with her.'

'So should I,' observed Violet meditatively; 'and I think I'll do it too. She is a kind old woman, and she was very nice to me the last time I saw her. After all, one can but be turned away from the door.'

Mrs. Stanton, being aware that her daughter was quite as likely as not to do this very unconventional thing, protested with some warmth.

'My dear child, what are you thinking of! You don't know Lady Elizabeth nearly well enough to call upon her without me, and for the present they must feel that the kindest thing we can do is to leave them alone. Now I do hope and trust that you won't be so silly as to give offence to people who may still be of the greatest service to you. It is no small matter for a girl in your position to have made friends with Lady Hartlepool, and I wouldn't for the world have her suppose that you are one of those horrid garrison young women who will take an ell if you give them an inch.'

Violet never stood in need of any arguments to induce her to take her own way; but if she had required these, they would doubtless have been furnished to her by her mother. She was warm-hearted, she liked Lady Elizabeth Chaine and wanted to tell her that she was sorry for her; she was not much afraid of being mistaken for a garrison young woman, and she was certainly not to be deterred from acting as she might see fit by the dread of any such misconception. Accordingly, she walked down that afternoon to the stable-yard of her friend Mr. Wicks and told him that, if he had nothing better to do with that pony of his, he might harness him to a two-wheeled cart for her.

Fat Mr. Wicks, who was standing with his hands under his coat-tails, his legs very wide apart and a straw in his mouth, touched his hat, grinned and answered: 'Cert'nly, miss. Mind he don't get boltin' away with you, that's all. It'll do him good to get a bit of exercise, and I shan't charge you nothin' for your drive, without you was to let him down and break his knees.'

'Let him down!' echoed Violet, with ineffable scorn. 'I'm about as likely to do that as he is to bolt with me. If you say much more, I'll order a closed fly, and you may drive it yourself.'

Mr. Wicks chuckled. He took a personal and quasi-paternal pride in Miss Stanton, who had learnt to ride and drive in her childhood under his tutelage, and who, as he was fond of declaring, could now teach him more about the management of horses than he could teach her.

'Now that's what I call a real lady,' he said presently to his head groom, as she drove away in her pony-cart; 'one of the right sort. Which there ain't too many of 'em about nowadays, I can tell you.'

'Some calls her a bit fast,' remarked the man, with an air of meditative impartiality.

'Do they indeed, Chawles?' returned Mr. Wicks, fixing his little black eyes upon his subordinate; 'you don't tell me so! Well, the very next party as you hears makin' that observation, I should take it as a favour if you'd beg him to step inside o' my office and repeat it to me. If I don't convince him he's a liar in less than a couple of minutes—ah, and indooce him to confess it likewise—why, my name ain't Peter Wicks, that's all. Fast indeed! There's some folks as is a deal too fast in talkin' about their betters and a deal too slow in doin' of their own work, I know. And, not to flatter you, Chawles, you're one of 'em. Now just you go and dress that there grey horse, and look alive about it. D'you think I ain't got nothin' better to do than stand here all day listenin' to your foolish talk?'

The rebuked Charles was by no means the only person in St. Albyn's who ventured to think Violet Stanton a little fast in her conduct, nor in truth was she fairly entitled to complain of that judgment; but, on the other hand, Mr. Wicks was not her only champion. There was something about her—her unaffected honesty, perhaps—which had earned her staunch friends in all ranks of society; and amongst the latter was Lady Elizabeth Chaine, into whose presence she was admitted shortly after this, and who kissed her affectionately, saying:

'My dear, how good of you to take pity upon a lonely old woman! Not a soul has been near me for the last age. Is it that they look upon us as a disgrace to the neighbourhood, do you think? Or is it only that they are afraid to call because they are too stupid to know what they ought to say?'

'I believe I am one of the stupid people who don't know what to say,' answered Violet, reddening slightly—for it occurred to her all of a sudden that she had undertaken a somewhat difficult task—'I only wanted to tell you that I was sorry, as everybody else is, about your dreadful trouble.'

'Well, that is quite the right thing to say,' Lady Elizabeth declared; 'you couldn't say more or say it better. Of course ours is a very dreadful trouble; it has made us all more or less ill, and I think it will kill my husband. But sitting alone and brooding over it doesn't make it any the easier to bear. It is a relief to be able to talk about something else.'

It is, of course, a relief to us all when we are in trouble to have our thoughts diverted; but a capacity for diversion is usually taken as a sign of heartlessness, and for some time past poor Lady Elizabeth had neither dared to speak of anything except the family humiliation, nor to look as if there could be room for other subjects in her mind. She now grew quite cheerful while listening to the not very varied programme of Violet's daily occupations and amusements and laughed heartily at the girl's confession that she would like to live in a country where it was always winter, so that hunting might never cease.

'So would Anne Hartlepool, I believe,' said she; 'but then Anne was never pretty, which makes a difference. By the way, I had a letter from her yesterday, in which she inquired after you. I am going to take care that Anne doesn't forget you,' continued the old lady, nodding at her young friend. 'I did quite hope and intend to carry you off to London next season and show you what the outer world was like; but now I must find a substitute. Come what may, the remainder of my life can only be spent in strict seclusion.'

Indeed it was not possible to forget for very long the shadow which hung over that afflicted household. Lady Elizabeth was rather more amply provided with courage and philosophy than most people; but she could discern no encouraging promise in the future, and she could not help crying a little when she began to speak of the present.

'If it were not for Wilfrid, I don't know what I should do!' she exclaimed; 'he manages to be some comfort to his father, but I can't. No one who hasn't been through it can imagine how trying it is to spend hour after hour in the company of a silent Christian martyr. You must forgive me for talking like this; I know I ought not to do it; but I have never been as good or as religious as my husband, and for the life of me I can't comprehend what satisfaction there can be in sitting all day with an open Bible upon one's knees and dying by inches. Dear me! the men in the Bible didn't behave like that—except, perhaps, Eli; and I suppose he wouldn't have broken his neck if he hadn't happened to overbalance himself.'

Lady Elizabeth's impatience was not in-excusable. Mr. Chaine was bearing his sorrow bravely in a certain sense ; but he did not seem to realise that other people might be no less worthy of compassion than he was, and there could be no doubt but that he was killing himself. At that very moment the doctor was affirming as much to Wilfrid, with whom he was holding a serious colloquy in the entrance hall.

' Unless you can contrive to rouse him by some means or other, he will slip through our fingers one of these fine mornings from sheer lack of vital force,' the local practitioner was saying. 'The whole College of Physicians couldn't do anything for a man in his state. There is really no sufficient reason why he should not live for another ten 'years, if he wished to live ; but the mischief of it is that he doesn't.'

Wilfrid shook his head and sighed. 'I am doing my best,' he replied—and indeed, to all appearance, so he was.

With a countenance expressive of befitting grief and resignation, he accompanied the doctor to the door, thus becoming aware of the pony-cart which was waiting outside. Miss Stanton, the butler informed him, in answer to his inquiry, was with her ladyship; so presently he strolled into the drawing-room, not so much because he had any particular wish to see Miss Stanton, as because, like his mother, he was growing terribly weary of seeing nobody at all. Miss Stanton, however, impressed him favourably when he did see her; for he was struck by her beauty, by her natural ease of manner and by the correct cut of her costume. Women did not, as a rule, interest him much; he had a poor opinion both of their moral and of their intellectual qualities, and he had no chivalrous instincts. To him a pretty face was, of course, a pretty face, and therefore pleasanter to look at than a plain one; but it would have been no great sacrifice to him to relinquish all future association with the feminine division of his own class. Nevertheless, he recognised that, under

his present altered circumstances, it would
behove him to marry before he was much
older, and while he was exchanging commonplaces with Violet Stanton the idea crossed
his mind that she would make a very credit-
able sort of *châtelaine.*   It was only a passing
idea, and it is only mentioned now because
it recurred to him at a later period, with
consequences which affect the course of this
narrative.   For the moment other subjects
of more pressing importance claimed his
attention.

Chief among these was the paramount
necessity of silencing Jessie Viccars, from whom
he had recently received more than one letter
and who, as it appeared, was not so discouraged
as she ought to have been by the catastrophe
which had put an end to her negotiations with
John.   She still demanded the fulfilment of
promises which could not now be shown to
have been granted to her; she still threatened
a descent upon Chaine Court, and she still
unquestionably had it in her power to inflict
serious annoyance upon Mr. Chaine's heir-pre-

sumptive. It was of this that Wilfrid was thinking as he helped Violet into her pony-cart, and this, no doubt, it was that gave him an air of abstraction which earned her approval.

' It is nice of him to be so distressed about his brother,' the girl mused, after she had taken leave of him ; ' it isn't everybody who would be distressed at coming into a property like this. The younger one was rather nice too ; but I expect he is as selfish as other young men. He doesn't seem to have thought it worth while to come home and cheer up his parents.'

Selfishness, as everybody knows, is of various kinds. More often than not it defeats its own ends ; but nothing so painful and fatal was likely to occur in the case of Wilfrid Chaine, who possessed the advantage which is not common to all selfish people of knowing exactly what he wanted. A few days later he made some excuse for running up to London, and there sought an interview with Mrs. Viccars, who gave him comparatively little trouble.

'Certainly I have not written to you, Jessie,' said he sternly, in answer to the volley of reproaches with which she greeted him; 'knowing what I now know of the use to which you put my letters, I shall scarcely be guilty of the folly of corresponding with you again. My poor brother, when you saw fit to betray me to him, acted as any gentleman would have done; he simply handed your precious document over to me, and I burnt it.'

'You shouldn't have driven me to desperation,' returned the woman sullenly. 'As for Mr. John, what he did was to ask me for proofs, and I let him have them. I don't see why it was like a gentleman to hand you over what didn't belong to him.'

'Very likely you don't, my dear Jessie, and you are probably also unaware that, by the law of the land, a letter belongs to its writer. Anyhow, that letter no longer exists; so that it will be interesting to hear what step you propose to take next.'

She could but reiterate her menace of telling all to Mr. Chaine; and, formidable though this was, Wilfrid easily persuaded her that it was nothing of the sort. His father, he said, would probably refuse to see her and, even if he did see her, would not believe her story. However, she might please herself in the matter.

'You have chosen to fight me, Jessie, and I never refuse a fight, though I am not given to provoking one. You must be very well aware that, after what has occurred, I shall not be such a fool as to marry you ; but, as I consider that you have still some sort of claim upon me, I will undertake to make you an allowance of £200 a year henceforth. This, I need hardly add, will be conditional upon your good behaviour. The moment that you attempt to annoy or persecute me in any way your allowance will cease, and a very little consideration will show you that you can by no possibility gain anything in exchange.'

He had thought it very likely that his offer would be accepted; but he was somewhat surprised when it was accepted almost without a protest. The truth was that Jessie Viccars

no longer wished to become his wife. He had
succeeded in making her hate and despise him
so thoroughly that she would have felt it impossible to spend the rest of her days with him
even if he had had ten times his prospective
wealth. She would fain also have refused the
income so contemptuously flung to her; but
she was without friends and without resources.

'I'll take your money until I can see my
way to earning my own living,' were her
valedictory words; 'after all, it's no charity,
it's only the payment of a debt. I don't want
ever to see or speak to you again; but I may
have something to say about you one of these
days.'

'As you please, my dear,' returned Wilfrid
affably; 'you know what the consequences of
any indiscretion on your part will be.'

He had little fear of her proving indiscreet,
and he returned to Chaine Court that evening
with a light heart. Everything had gone so
wonderfully well with him of late that he had
some right to look upon himself as one of
Fortune's favourites.

CHAPTER XIX

GOOD NEWS

IN these days—and possibly things may not have been so very different as we are wont to imagine even in the distant days before railways, telegraphs and the penny post were invented to disturb the peace of the world— most of us suffer from the incessant hustle and bustle which causes us to waste our few spare minutes in sighing for rest. Yet, as a matter of fact, rest does not agree with us; the exceptional persons who obtain it usually die of it, and perhaps there is nothing quite so hopeless or terrible as an absolutely uneventful existence.

There came now to the inhabitants of Chaine Court a period, lasting through many months, which was marked by no important event whatsoever; and why this did not cause

the death of old Mr. Chaine was what Wilfrid
wondered every day with increasing impatience.
He himself was weary beyond all power of
expression ; the consolations of religion, which
apparently sustained his father, were not open
to him ; he did not care for the pursuits which
had interested John; yet he could not go away,
because he was supposed to be taking John's
place and because both his parents implored
him not to leave them.   He did once remark
tentatively to his mother that a brief holiday
might recruit his strength; but Lady Elizabeth
would not hear of such a thing.

'My dear boy,' she exclaimed, 'your father
would be shocked and horrified if it were
suggested to him that you are capable of
wishing to be amused ! He already suspects
dimly that you would like to escape from this
appalling monotony, and if his suspicions are
confirmed, there is no saying what he may not
do. No ; you must bear your burden—perhaps
it won't be for long—and in due season you will
reap your reward.   Of course the monotony *is*
appalling ; I'm sure I find it so myself !   But

nothing can break it, except the news of John's arrest, and I suppose we ought really to be thankful that nothing has happened or is likely to happen. For my own part, I can't be thankful enough that you are in the house. If you went away, I should simply be driven to confide my woes to my maid—which is always a sign of the approaching imbecility of old age.'

Lady Elizabeth was very sorry for herself, as well she might be; but in truth the human intercourse for which she longed was not entirely restricted to the conversation of her son and the funereal orations of her husband. She had a voluminous correspondence which kept her busy during a great part of the day, and in the course of the afternoon it not unfrequently happened that Violet Stanton dropped in to take a cup of tea with her. The friendship which sprang up between the old and the young lady was of a kind which would probably be more common if more opportunities were afforded for its development, because each was able to give the other

something that had a real, although scarcely a
tangible value. Association upon terms of
equality with youth is always stimulating and
invigorating to age; while age, if only it can
avoid being pedantic and commonplace, should
always be able to interest youth. Lady Elizabeth, who had lived for many years in the
world, knew quite a large number of things
which Violet did not know, and she had an
innocent, matter-of-course way of alluding to
the manners and customs of modern society
which tickled as well as edified her visitor.
So, as the summer faded into autumn and
the leaves began to flutter down from the
trees around Chaine Court, these two became
tolerably constant companions and arrived at
a point of mutual regard which was not without subsequent influence upon the career of
one of them.

One afternoon it occurred to Violet to inquire after Hubert, with whom she had half
hoped to renew her acquaintance in the latter
part of the year, and the answer which she received was something of a disappointment to her.

'Oh, didn't I tell you?' said Lady Elizabeth. 'He has been sent off to the Cape with
his regiment. Foreign service is not exactly
what he likes, and under other circumstances
I dare say he would have tried to effect an
exchange; but as things are now, it was perhaps better that he should go, poor boy!
One may hope that by the time he returns
people will have ceased to point him out as
John Chaine's brother.'

So there was an end of any incipient
romance which may have been forming itself
in Miss Violet's mind. She had not, of
course, been enamoured of the young soldier;
but, equally of course, she had not been ignorant of the fact that she had attracted his
profound admiration, and she felt that his
departure for a distant colony, without even
running down to Southshire for a day in order
to take leave, was in some sort a slight upon
her, as well as a neglect of filial duty. Lady
Elizabeth, however, did not seem to resent
that omission. Lady Elizabeth, who liked a
great many people and was kind to every-

body, really loved only one person in the world, and so long as Wilfrid remained with her, her maternal cravings had a sufficient outlet. She sometimes thought — recent events having so completely deprived her of ambition—that it would be rather nice if Wilfrid and Violet were to take a fancy to one another, and she noticed without regret that the former was very apt to drop in casually about tea-time on the days when Miss Stanton happened to be there.

But when the hunting began in earnest Miss Stanton's visits to Chaine Court naturally became less frequent. For the possessor of a single horse to hunt three days a week is what most hunting men would unhesitatingly pronounce to be an impossibility; yet, by judicious management, there is more work to be got out of one horse than most hunting men suspect: moreover, the good-natured Mr. Wicks (upon an honourable understanding that the matter should not be talked about) was willing to let a certain customer of his have a mount from time to time at the

nominal figure of seven and sixpence. Thus
Wilfrid's chronic boredom was not often
relieved by a meeting with the young lady
whose manners and appearance had earned
his appreciation, while poor Lady Elizabeth's
afternoons were spent for the most part in
uninterrupted solitude.

It was on a chilly morning in early winter
that a piece of news reached her which not
only gave her something to think and talk
about, but which it would have been sheer
affectation on her part to treat as unwelcome.
She had eaten her breakfast and had almost
finished perusing her correspondence when a
message was brought to her from Mr. Chaine,
who now seldom left his bedroom, to the
effect that he would be glad if she would
come upstairs for a few minutes. She found
the old man somewhat flushed and agitated,
but she noticed at once that his face had lost
its habitual expression of despondent resignation.

'Elizabeth,' said he gravely, 'something
has happened which might have tempted us

to repine a year ago. I do not think that we have any right or reason to repine now; although, as Christian people, we cannot but entertain some terrible misgivings with regard to our son John, who has been suddenly called to his account.'

He gave her a letter, bearing an American stamp and written in the clerkly, unmeaning hand affected by nine out of ten citizens of the United States. Its contents, over which she ran her eye hastily, fully confirmed her husband's startling announcement :—

'SIR—I have the regret to inform you that I have this day been present at the interment of an Englishman who until lately was known to us as William Brown, but who confided to me upon his deathbed that his true name was John Chaine, and who requested me to place myself in communication with you as soon as he should have breathed his last. After defraying necessary expenses for doctor, funeral, etc., there remained in the possession of the deceased a sum of 450 dollars (£95 : 12 : 6), for which please find draft enclosed, and acknowledge receipt to the undersigned.

'The late John Chaine, otherwise William Brown, was engaged in agricultural operations in this neighbourhood when he met with an accident, through his horse falling with him, and received injuries which resulted in his death. I understood from him that he had been compelled to leave England and change his name in consequence of his having unfortunately killed a man in a fair fight. He wished you to know that he was innocent of malicious intention and ignorant at the time of what he had done. I was also to convey an assurance of unaltered affection to his wife and the other members of his family.

'I mail to you to-day a packet containing his watch and chain, signet-ring and two scarf-pins, which I trust will reach you safely.

'Should you desire further details, I shall be happy to furnish you with them, and

'I am, Sir,

'Respectfully yours,

'BENJN. S. WHARTON.

'Jamestown, Dakota, U.S.A.'

Well, poor John had never been anything but a most unsatisfactory son, and that his disappearance from his native land might be final was what his mother had necessarily regarded as a thing to be hoped and prayed for; still she was, after all, his mother, so that she dropped a few natural tears upon the concise statement of Mr. Benjamin S. Wharton.

'I suppose it must be true,' she said at length.

'It is difficult to doubt the veracity of a man who encloses a cheque for £95,' replied her husband gravely. 'You mean, perhaps, that it might be worth John's while to circulate a false report of his death; but I question whether he could afford to pay so large a sum for his security, nor do I think it likely that he would have parted with his watch and the other trinkets which have been forwarded to me. Of course I will write to this Mr. Wharton and request fuller particulars: the truth of his statement, however, seems to me to be as good as proved. I should be a hypocrite if I were to pretend that my sorrow is not lightened by our bereavement.'

He was not a hypocrite, although he sometimes talked rather like one. As for Lady Elizabeth, she seldom tried to conceal her sentiments and always failed egregiously when she made the attempt.

'It is better for him to be dead than to live on in the backwoods as a fugitive from justice,' she remarked, after a pause.

'I hope so,' returned Mr. Chaine somewhat gloomily.

'And I am sure he was telling the truth, poor fellow, when he said that he had no malicious intention of killing that unfortunate man.'

'I hope so,' repeated Mr. Chaine, with the same dubious intonation.

'Well, at any rate, it isn't for us to believe the worst about him, now that he is gone. Wilfrid, you know, has maintained all along that the catastrophe was a pure accident. This will be a blow to Wilfrid—and to poor Ida too.'

'I scarcely think so, Elizabeth : what John's parents are compelled to recognise as a cause for thankfulness cannot very well present itself in any other light to his brother or his widow. Still the news will probably be a shock to Ida ; for one cannot tell what groundless hopes she may not have cherished secretly, poor thing ! I think you should lose no time in breaking it to her.'

Lady Elizabeth sighed. She hated agitating scenes, and, notwithstanding her conviction that Ida had never cared very much for John, she felt the awkwardness of having to say to anybody, 'I am happy to inform you that your husband is no more.' She knew her own sex well enough to be aware that there could be no foreseeing in what manner such an announcement would be received. At the same time, it was clearly incumbent upon her to say what must be said; so presently she went downstairs and ordered the carriage.

About an hour later she was at the White House and in the presence of her daughter-in-law, who almost immediately exclaimed, with nervous apprehension, 'You have come to tell me that you have heard something about John!'

Since her husband's disappearance Ida had led a life of seclusion which, combined with the natural anxiety from which she suffered, had been prejudicial to her health. Her complexion, always pale, was now livid; her cheek-bones had become prominent, and her great dark eyes had the eager, hunted look which is only produced by suspense. Lady Elizabeth was a little afraid of her : that is, she was afraid that the woman might go off into a fit of hysterics or otherwise cause inconvenience to innocent bystanders.

'My dear,' she said solemnly, 'you must try to compose yourself and to bear in mind that—that all things are ordered for the best. At least, one has always been taught that it is one's duty to think so ; and really, in such a case as poor John's, everybody must allow that death is by no means the worst thing that could have happened. As Mr. Chaine very truly says, what John's parents are obliged to acknowledge as a sort of blessing ought not to be rebelled against by——'

'Do you mean that John is dead ?' interrupted Ida.

Lady Elizabeth made a sign of assent. 'We have had a letter from America to-day which leaves us without any hope—without any doubt, I mean. His money and his watch have been returned to us. It seems that he was farming in one of those out-of-the-way places and that his horse threw him or fell with him. It is very sad; still, if you will think of it, what better fate was there open to him?'

'Thank God!' ejaculated the widow fervently.

The elder lady looked a trifle shocked. It was a comfort that there were to be no hysterics; yet she could not quite approve of such crudity of language. 'I am glad you take it in that way,' she remarked rather drily; 'we were dreading the effect of this news upon you.'

Ida made no immediate rejoinder. She admitted to herself that she ought, perhaps, to be sorry; but, on the other hand, she had ample excuses for not being sorry, and, like Mr. Chaine, she did not care to play the hypocrite.

'I suppose my feelings about it are very much the same as your own,' was all that she could finally plead in extenuation of her hard-heartedness.

'If they are, you must be very unhappy and a good deal ashamed,' answered Lady Elizabeth. 'Yet, after all, you have less reason to be ashamed than I have; for you did your duty to poor John, whereas I never did mine, I am afraid. Anyhow, we were neither of us to blame for his misfortunes, and we should probably not have seen his face again if he had lived for another half century : we must take what comfort we can from that thought.'

In truth, no relative of the late John Chaine stood in need of consolatory reflections. Even if they had loved him, they could hardly, under the circumstances, have deplored his demise ; and, as a matter of fact, he had not been lovable. When a man who is afflicted with red hair, an ugly face, disagreeable manners and a nasty temper sees fit to commit murder into the bargain, he tries human patience a little too highly ; nor is he fairly entitled to any deeper mourning than that which conventionality and the purveyors of black crape are willing to devote to his memory for a few months after his disappearance from these earthly scenes. Lady Elizabeth was capable of a vague sensation of remorse which was not incompatible with relief; but Ida, whose character was constructed upon different lines, was a poor hand at self-deception. Her husband had made himself detestable to her; he had forfeited every claim upon her regard by slaying—and, as she still believed, deliberately slaying—her only friend; she could not but rejoice that death had set her free for ever from one with whom, if she had only understood him a little better at the outset, she would herself infinitely rather have died than united her fate.

Of course she donned widow's weeds, and the servants at Chaine Court were put into sable liveries, and old Mr. Chaine ordered a hat-band for himself; but her health began to mend, as did that of her father-in-law, who not only adorned his hat in the manner mentioned, but proceeded to put it on and drove down to the White House for the purpose of assuring Ida that that residence would be hers for the remainder of her days. In course of time a second and somewhat more lengthy communication arrived from Mr. Wharton; the county was duly made aware that the deceased had, upon his death-bed, declared himself guiltless of a pre-meditated crime, and the universal verdict upon the whole tragic affair was that it had ended in a more satisfactory and less dis-creditable fashion than could have been anticipated.

If there had been a discordant note in this general and generous chorus of 'All's well that ends well,' it would probably have issued from the lips of Wilfrid, who, while rejoicing in the thought that John could not now take it into his head to return to England and make embarrassing revelations, was a little disappointed by his father's restoration to comparative vigour. But Wilfrid was a patient as well as a prudent man; so he held his peace and looked pleasant. He was also careful to ingratiate himself with Ida, little

as he liked the idea of being ultimately called
upon to pay two jointures out of his revenues
—which, so far as he could understand his
father's intentions, appeared to be the arrangement in prospect. That arrangement, he
thought, might be modified by the customary
limitations, and Mrs. John Chaine, being a
young and handsome woman, would very
probably marry again. Meanwhile, it was
as well to keep upon good terms with her;
for he had observed that she exercised considerable influence over an irritable old gentleman who knew no law save his own good
will and pleasure.

CHAPTER XX

THE DÉBUTANTE

WHETHER it is not better to live quite alone
than in the society of an uncongenial companion is a question to which most people
would give an affirmative answer without
much hesitation ; but then most people,
happily for themselves, do not know what
living quite alone means. Ida Chaine was
perhaps as well fitted by temperament to
lead a solitary existence as any human being
can be ; yet, during those long winter months
when the snow lay upon the ground, or
south-westerly gales raged among the bare
trees around her dwelling, with a sharp rattle
of rain against the windows, she felt more
than once that death had fewer terrors for
her than the interminable period of comfortable imprisonment to which she saw herself

condemned. She was, to be sure, free from
material anxieties; the man who had been
legally entitled to claim her as belonging to
him, and whose ultimate return she had dreaded
with an intensity almost amounting to panic,
lay dead and buried in distant Dakota; she
was her own mistress, and she was amply
provided for. But, somehow or other, these
seemed to be only negative blessings, and at
her time of life it was natural that she should
pine for something positive.

She did not find what she wanted in the
visits of her father, who came over to see her
every now and again and sat for a while
enunciating well-turned platitudes, with one
plump leg crossed over the other and a smile
of benevolent contentment upon his lips; she
did not find it in the amiable prattle of Lady
Elizabeth, with whom she had very little in
common, nor in the austere discourses of old
Mr. Chaine, although, upon the whole, he
interested her more than anybody else with
whom she was brought into contact at this
time. Old Mr. Chaine was as honest and

upright as he was narrow-minded ; there was
a suggestion of power and capacity in all that
he said and did which was not without a
certain fascination of its own, and he was full
of kindliness towards his daughter-in-law,
regarding himself as in some sense responsible
for the misfortunes that had come upon her ;
still he could scarcely be called sympathetic, and
he was often wearisome. Wilfrid would have
been pleased had he known how frequently, in
her hours of solitude, the widow's thoughts
reverted to that young lover of hers whom she
had seen fit to drive away from her upon the
eve of her marriage, and of whom no law,
human or divine, forbade her any longer to
dream. However, she heard nothing about
Arthur Mayne ; nor, for the matter of that,
had she any hope that his constancy could
have survived the very severe test to which it
had been put. She dreamt of him only because dreaming is an agreeable and innocent
occupation, and because she was so terribly at
a loss for occupations of any kind.

It was probably for the same reason that

she took to visiting the poor. She did not really enjoy visiting the poor and did not feel herself to be particularly adapted for the exercise of that form of benevolence; but, as she had plenty of pocket-money and was devoid of impertinence or self-righteousness, she soon acquired a fair share of popularity amongst her humbler neighbours. By this means also she became acquainted with the Miss Frasers, four good-humoured, plain-featured spinsters, who seemed to be resigned to the probable permanence of their spinster-hood, and of whose helpfulness the Vicar of the parish spoke in warm terms. Their father, Colonel Fraser, welcomed her kindly when she called, by their request, at Hatton Park, and refrained from any allusion to the painful circumstances which had placed him in possession of that desirable residence. Neither he nor his rather commonplace family added very much to Ida's interest in life; but she added greatly to theirs, and no doubt it was good for her to be roused out of her sombre musings from time to time by the rosy-cheeked

girls, who regarded her with that admiration
which rosy - cheeked young women usually
conceive for pale and melancholy ones.

Violet Stanton, without being open to the
reproach of being rosy-cheeked, sincerely admired Mrs. John Chaine and felt a great
curiosity with reference to that lady which she
would probably have endeavoured to gratify
by means of closer intercourse but for the
paramount claims of the Southshire foxhounds. During the hunting season Violet
practically ceased to exist for social purposes; so that nothing immediate came of
that favourable, though indecisive, impression
which she had produced upon the philosophic
Wilfrid. It was but seldom that she could
spare time for a hurried visit to Lady Elizabeth, and when she did drink tea at Chaine
Court, she did not meet the acknowledged
heir, for the very good reason that he was not
there. The chief advantage of being a philo-
sopher is that one learns by philosophy to
make the best of what cannot be helped, and
Mr. Chaine's unexpected recovery was at least

a blessing to his son, in so far as it gave the latter an excuse for absenting himself from home. Wilfrid was one of those somewhat exceptional men who like London all the year round ; he was always pretty sure of meeting acquaintances there, and he rejoiced as much in his return to club life as in his release from the tedium of that which belongs to a semi - inhabited country - house. Of Jessie Viccars he heard nothing, and in this agreeable transition period he doubtless forgot that there was such a person in the world as Miss Violet Stanton, who, for her part, returned the compliment. It may be truthfully said of Violet that, so long as she could hunt three days (and sometimes four) in the week, she asked no more of a world which is well known to be prolific in illusions and disappointments.

But one cannot hunt from January to December, and one must attempt to enjoy oneself in one way or another while crops are growing and hedges are green and cubs are attaining maturity. This was what Lady Hartlepool,

who made an abrupt descent upon Chaine
Court in the month of February, pointed out
to the young lady who had been fortunate
enough to acquire her interest and friendship.

'I shall send for you as soon as we move up
to London,' she said. 'Aunt Elizabeth wants
me to present you and take you about; and
even if you don't find that sort of thing
particularly good fun at the time, you will be
glad to have been through it afterwards. Besides, it may give you the chance of meeting
somebody whom you wouldn't mind marrying
—which, of course, is the real meaning of it all.
Match-making is rather more in Aunt Elizabeth's line than it is in mine; still I could
name at least a dozen men who would do very
well for you and whom you might like.'

Lady Hartlepool was plain in speech, as she
was in face. She liked to call a spade a spade;
but as this was her natural habit, it had not
that offensiveness with which we have all sad
reason to be familiar, now that plain speaking
has become fashionable. Violet found her

anything but offensive, and accepted her invitation with unfeigned gratitude and pleasure.

'One out of the dozen is sure to suit me,' she answered, laughing; 'for I am not a bit particular. There are only two things which I should consider essential in a husband: he must be rich, and he must know how to ride.'

'Oh, is that all?' said Lady Hartlepool drily. 'Well there are a fairish number of bachelors who can ride; but the rich ones are not quite so plentiful. However, we must see what we can do, and I shall be able to scheme on your behalf with a clear conscience, because I am sure that the man who marries you won't repent of his choice.'

This was a rather bold assertion to make; but Lady Hartlepool's assertions and actions were apt to be bold, though she committed herself to neither in haste. She had taken a liking to this country-bred girl, and her likings were never half-hearted, nor were her promises ever broken.

Thus it came to pass that, shortly after
Easter, Violet and her modest supply of
luggage were deposited at the door of that
imposing mansion in Park Lane which the
late Lord Hartlepool had caused to be erected
when the discovery of coal upon his property
in the north had brought him such a vast
accession of wealth that he hardly knew what
to do with it. The present owner of the
coals and the mansion, a homely, middle-aged
personage, with a bald head and short, red-
dish whiskers, welcomed his wife's protegée
hospitably, but was too busy to take much
notice of her. Lord Hartlepool was a great
man because he was so rich, and a busy
man chiefly because such a formidable number of people desired to transfer a portion
of his riches from his pocket to their own.
Generally speaking, they succeeded; but their
demands required investigation, and as Lord
Hartlepool took a tolerably active part in
politics, his life, when he was in London,
was one of incessant hurry and bustle.
Violet had been a week under his roof be-

fore she exchanged a dozen words with him.

Not, to be sure, that his neglect in any way distressed her. She herself was uncommonly busy during that week, and had more important persons and things to think about than an elderly member of the House of Lords. The sensations of a young girl who has suddenly been transported from the depths of the country into the midst of that heterogeneous collection of human beings which constitutes what in these days has come to be known as London society must, one may assume, be not unlike those of a small boy when he is first sent to school. It would be interesting to know (but nobody ever will know, because they are so much more reticent than small boys) how the whole thing strikes them : whether they are dazzled by the glitter and ostentation of it, or whether their natural, healthy instincts are shocked by the vulgarity which, unhappily, must be acknowledged to be its dominant feature. In any case, it seems certain that strange discoveries and revelations must await them at every turn, and that, although they may have heard or read this, that, and the other about the cynicism of the fashionable world, they must be a little surprised—as indeed we all are—to find that the accounts which have been given of it are not in the least exaggerated. Violet, for her part, had always professed to hold somewhat cynical opinions, and if she was shocked by the conversation of some of Lady Hartlepool's friends, she did not look so. The ceremony of her presentation to her Sovereign was, of course, rather an ordeal; but she was well coached and got through it quite creditably, not forgetting to make the requisite number of curtseys to the surrounding Royalties. After that, there really was not much to throw a well-balanced mind off its hinges, nor did Miss Stanton display any of that bewilderment which, to tell the truth, her sponsor had expected of her.

'You seem to take all this as a matter of course,' Lady Hartlepool remarked in an almost aggrieved tone, as they were driving home from a ball together late one night, or rather early one morning. 'I should have thought you would have been either delighted or disgusted.'

'But so I am,' answered Violet; 'I am delighted. If I hadn't seen it with my own eyes, I could never have believed that anybody would spend such a lot of money upon a ball. And the flowers were exquisite, and the music was first-rate, and the partners were— well, the partners were pretty tolerable. Oh, yes; I am quite delighted.'

'I suppose,' sighed Lady Hartlepool, 'it is because I am growing old that I can't make head or tail of you young people. I don't see what business you have to take things so coolly; but perhaps, after all, it is just as well that you should.'

'I don't take a good run with the hounds coolly,' Violet returned. 'There is some excitement about that; but what real difference does it make whether a man who pays you laborious compliments is a grandee or only a humble cavalry officer? At St. Albyn's

I dance with cavalry officers, and here I dance
with grandees. There is nothing that I can
see to choose between them, except that these
people are mostly rich, whereas the others are
mostly poor.'

'But I thought you attached such importance to riches.'

'Certainly I do ; and that was my reason
for dancing four times this evening with Sir
Harvey Amherst, who is a gay widower of
nearer fifty than forty, and who as good as
told me that he was looking out for a second
wife. Sir Harvey lives on the other side of
the county, as you know ; but he sometimes
comes out with our hounds, and he goes
straight. Once, when he was away from
home, I went with a picnic party to Amherst
Place, and I had a look at the stables. There
were eighteen loose boxes—no less than that !'

'I see,' said Lady Hartlepool resignedly,
'that you have nothing to learn. It only
remains for me to ask Sir Harvey Amherst
to dinner — which shall be done without
unnecessary delay.'

There certainly was no reason why that
wealthy and popular baronet should not be
asked to dinner, and if the decree of Providence or the inclination of the persons
chiefly concerned should eventually bring
about a union between him and a girl from
his native county whose face was her fortune,
there would be every reason for congratulating
them both.   It was true that he was no longer
young; but then he made himself look as
young as he could, and he had plenty of
money and no children.

'She might easily do a great deal worse,
and I suppose one ought not to blame her
for taking a more practical view of life than
girls of her age generally do,' mused Lady
Hartlepool, whose own marriage, which had
scarcely been one of inclination, had turned
out satisfactorily enough.

Sir Harvey Amherst, therefore, was duly
bidden to her next feast and availed himself
of the invitation.   He was a slim, dapper
gentleman, whose clothes fitted him beautifully and who was still handsome, notwith-

standing the crow's-feet at the corners of his
eyes. His hair might possibly have been
gray if he had allowed Nature to have her
own way with him; but there could be no
deception about his lithe, youthful figure; and
his manners, as everybody admitted, were
quite charming. He was decidedly attentive
to Miss Stanton throughout the evening, and
before he went away he took occasion to put
a few questions to his hostess with regard to
her young friend's origin and belongings
which sounded business-like.

A certain cousin of Lady Hartlepool's who,
as chance would have it, was also among her
guests that evening, took note of these things,
and remarked to her : 'This is really too bad
of you, Anne ; I gave you credit for higher
principles than to throw a child like Miss
Stanton at the head of an old fogey like
Amherst.'

'I am not throwing her at anybody's head,'
returned Lady Hartlepool ; 'and as for my
principles, I suspect that they would compare
favourably with yours. Moreover, I may tell

you that Miss Stanton was especially confided to my care by your mother, who is quite as much responsible for anything that may happen to her while she is in London as I can be.'

'So I understand,' answered Wilfrid, smiling; 'but if you think that my mother would approve of the match that you are trying to get up, you make a mistake. I can speak with some confidence upon the point, because I had a long letter from home a day or two ago in which it was impressed upon me that I ought to pay my respects to the young lady for whom you and my mother are jointly responsible. Would it surprise you to hear that my mother wishes me to come forward in the character of a rival to the sprightly and venerable Amherst?'

'It would not particularly surprise me; but if you mean to do as you are told, you will have to look for support to Aunt Elizabeth, not to me,' said Lady Hartlepool bluntly; for she did not like Wilfrid, and had never pretended to do so.

'Oh,' answered the latter, with a laugh, 'if I do as I am told, it won't be out of a spirit of obedience, and I shall rely exclusively upon the personal merits to which you are pleased to be blind. It is a good deal more likely, though, that I shall modestly stand aside and allow you to carry out your immoral project. The essential and innate immorality of your sex, of which I am always receiving fresh proofs, alarms me so much that I shudder at the bare idea of matrimony.'

Lady Hartlepool said she was glad to hear it; but she did not quite believe it, and, noticing subsequently that Wilfrid took the trouble to engage Miss Stanton in conversation for a matter of ten minutes or so, she judged it advisable to address a few precautionary remarks to the latter.

'I don't know how that cousin of mine strikes you,' said she in her abrupt way; 'but to my mind he is a shifty, untrustworthy sort of fellow. He used always to be trying to put a spoke in his elder brother's wheel, and I didn't half like his damaging evidence at the

inquest. He might easily have made out a
much better case if he had been so inclined.
Poor John was worth a dozen of him, and so
is Hubert, for that matter.'

'I never saw much of any of them,'
answered Violet indifferently. 'I liked the
youngest best, because he knew something
about the management of horses ; but this
one seems to be rather clever and amusing.
Lady Elizabeth talks of him as if he were
a sort of paragon.'

'Aunt Elizabeth is the easiest person in the
world to humbug ; she knows no more about
men than she does about horses. Wilfrid may
be amusing to some people, though he doesn't
amuse me, and I don't deny that he is clever ;
but I must say that personally I should prefer
Sir Harvey Amherst, in spite of his dyed hair.'

Violet laughed, understanding quite well
what was meant and being, perhaps, not
averse to the suggestion that she had secured
a second admirer at so small an expenditure
of pains. What woman does object to ad-
mirers ?

'Oui, femmes, quoiqu' on puisse dire,
Vous avez le fatal pouvoir
De nous jeter par un sourire
Dans l'ivresse ou dans le désespoir,'

says Alfred de Musset; but the power spoken
of by the poet is but transient (as indeed are
the intoxication and despair mentioned as its
consequences), and women are probably wise
to make the most of it while it lasts. Violet
Stanton, like the miller of Dee, was in the
happy position of caring for nobody, while she
was more fortunate than he, inasmuch as it
appeared that more than one person cared for
her. Without either liking or disliking Wilfrid
Chaine, she would have been willing to grant
him some measure of encouragement had he
come forward to beg for it; but, as a matter of
fact, she saw very little of him for a long time
after this, whereas she saw a good deal of Sir
Harvey Amherst, who was continually placing
himself in her path and who did what he
could to render her those services which are
always appreciated by her sex. He would
have been rather disagreeably surprised if he
had known that Violet regarded him simply as

an amiable old gentleman ; but possibly he might have been reassured had he also known that, in her opinion, an amiable old gentleman was as desirable a husband as another. Of course he was apt to be wearisome at times and his affectation of juvenility was a little comic ; yet, on the other hand, he rode straight to hounds and he had eighteen loose boxes in his stables.

CHAPTER XXI

SIR HARVEY AMHERST

IF a general plebiscite could be taken in order
to decide what are the constituent elements of
earthly happiness, the chief of these would
probably be pronounced to be health; since
the lot of a robust navvy is unquestionably
preferable to that of a debilitated duke or
millionaire. Wealth, it may be surmised,
would come in a good second, while success
and popularity might run a dead heat for the
third place, and possibly, as a concession to
moralists, a clear conscience might be thrown
in amongst other minor desiderata. Sir
Harvey Amherst, who possessed each and all
of these blessings, was rightly accounted a
happy man; and, in view of the ingratitude
which characterises the human race, it is
satisfactory to be able to add that he himself

concurred in the universal verdict. He had, it is true, a few things left to wish for—otherwise he could hardly have been happy—but none of them were unattainable, and he had a comforting conviction that, even if they should prove so, he would manage to get on pretty well without them.

At the time when he was introduced to Violet Stanton he happened to be in want of a wife; indeed it was almost his duty to select one, seeing that he had great possessions and no heir of his body. In early life he had married a lady of high rank who had been chosen for him by his parents; but this lady, after lingering on for many years as a childless invalid, had now gone to her rest, and it was his intention to marry a second time for his own pleasure. There really was no occasion for him to contract another noble alliance; his position was too high a one to stand in need of added glories, and he had come to the conclusion that Miss Stanton's pretty face placed her, so far as he was concerned, upon a level with any woman in England. It was, of course, necessary that she should be a lady; but he had ascertained that her belongings were quite decent. If he was a little more confident of obtaining her consent to the proposed arrangement than a modest man would have been, it may be pleaded in extenuation that he had never since his schooldays passed through any experiences of a nature to make him modest and that, in truth, very few of the girls with whom he was acquainted would have been so blind to their own interests as to refuse him. Moreover, Violet was, to all appearance, pleased and flattered by his attentions, which were paid with deliberation and delicacy.

'I wonder,' he said to her one afternoon, when he had met her, in obedience to a previous appointment, at Sandown and was escorting her, by her request, towards the paddock, 'whether I could induce you and Mrs. Stanton to pay me a visit at Amherst Place during the summer. It is within easy reach of you, and perhaps you would kindly pardon the shortcomings of a bachelor establishment. I shall get my sister to come down and stay with me, so that Mrs. Stanton won't be without a hostess,' he added, to show that he was not oblivious of the proprieties.

'I think we should both like it very much, thank you,' replied Violet. 'Of course I can't answer for mamma; but as a general rule she enjoys staying with people—whereas, as a general rule, there is nothing that I so cordially detest.'

'May I venture to accept that as a compliment?' asked Sir Harvey insinuatingly.

'Oh yes, if you choose to look upon it in that light. I once visited Amherst Place as a humble tripper, and I remember wishing with all my heart at the time that the owner of those stables would invite me to spend a few days with him and let me ride his horses.'

The owner of the stables assumed a gratified smile. 'I assure you, Miss Stanton,' said he, 'that you are more than welcome to ride and kill any horse in my possession, with one or two exceptions; and I only make those exceptions because I would a great deal rather die than allow any horse in my possession to kill you.'

'That is as much as to say that you don't believe I can ride,' returned the ungrateful young woman. 'Well, I think I may safely promise not to kill any animal of yours, and if you will kindly put me up on one of the exceptional ones, I hope I shall be able to convince you that there is no occasion for alarm on my account.'

Sir Harvey explained that sheer lack of strength, not lack of skill, might cause the best lady-rider in the world to be overpowered by a headstrong brute, adding, 'I am by no means a first-class horseman myself, and very likely you might succeed in cases where I am obliged to submit to failure ; but, for all that, I couldn't consent to let *you* run any risk. I must beg you, as a personal favour, not to ride three of the hunters whom you will see in my stable ; all the others will be quite at your disposal.'

'Well, we will see about it,' was all that Violet would concede in response to this touching appeal. 'My own conviction is that nothing very terrible can happen to anybody who knows how to stick to the saddle, and I have never been thrown yet.'

'I almost wish that you had been,' Sir Harvey declared. 'As for me, I have parted company with my saddle again and again, and probably it is just as well for me that I have lost the self-confidence with which I was blessed once upon a time.'

He was proceeding to employ some of those arguments which, unanswerable though they are, never have produced, and never will produce, the slightest impression upon the mind of a tyro, when his eloquence was interrupted by a smartly-dressed, sunburnt young man, who bowed to his companion, saying—

'How do you do, Miss Stanton? Anne told me you had gone off to the paddock; so I thought I would take the liberty of following you and claiming acquaintance.'

For some reason or other which she was unable to account for, the colour mounted into Violet's cheeks. Perhaps it was only surprise

that had caused her to redden, and probably
that was the impression which she desired to
convey to the new-comer when she exclaimed:
'How you startled me! I thought you were
at the Cape of Good Hope, or some such
place.'

'I was there about a month ago,' answered
Hubert Chaine, displaying his white teeth;
'but now, Heaven be praised! I am here.
I've exchanged into the 90th Hussars, and
I'm quartered at Hounslow, I'm thankful to
say. It was almost worth while to leave
one's native land for the pleasure of getting
back again. So you're doing a London season
under the wing of old Anne, I hear. I'm
awfully glad of it, because I expect I shall
be able to run up to town pretty often.'

'That will be very nice indeed,' said Violet
gravely. 'I'm afraid I shan't profit much
personally by your visits though, for I shall
soon have to begin thinking about returning
home.'

'Oh, not yet awhile,' protested the young
man; 'I'm sure Anne wouldn't hear of it—

she isn't half a bad sort, you know, old Anne
—and you can't possibly want to be in Southshire out of the hunting season. Although,'
he added ingenuously, 'I shall have to go
down there myself before long to see the old
people, I suppose.'

Sir Harvey Amherst had listened to the
above dialogue with some little impatience.
He gathered from it that this rather forward
boy was the youngest son of his old friend
and neighbour Mr. Chaine, and he was about
to address a few patronising words to the
intruder, preparatory to getting rid of him,
when he was touched on the elbow by a sporting peer, who had something important to
say to him. Sir Harvey, though no longer
a racing man, had once been among the most
prominent patrons of the turf, and his opinion
upon knotty points was still often requested
and always respected. He was not only
called upon for his opinion now, but was
detained so long before he could enunciate
it that, by the time that he was set at liberty,
his charge and her young friend were nowhere

to be seen. Sir Harvey was somewhat annoyed
by his failure to discover them; but in reality
they were not far away, nor, if he had overheard their conversation, would he have found
anything in it of a nature to cause him disquietude.

'The fact is,' Hubert was saying, as they
strolled away together across the grass, quite
forgetting to inspect the horses in the paddock,
'that I rather funk facing the old folks. I
haven't seen the governor since all this terrible
business about poor old John happened, and
something will have to be said about it.
Then, if I say what I think, I shall be pretty
sure to give offence; because my view certainly
won't be the same as his.'

'But there isn't room for much difference
of opinion upon the subject, is there?' said
Violet.

'Well, yes; I think there is. Between
you and me, I don't believe that John committed that murder; he wasn't at all the sort
of chap to do a thing of that kind. He might
have thrashed the fellow—and serve him jolly

well right if he had, most likely!—but he wouldn't have killed him.'

'He may have killed him unintentionally.'

'What! throttled him unintentionally? No fear! The man who killed Fraser meant to kill him; and that's why I'm sure John never did it. You may depend upon it that what occurred was this: he knocked the beggar down, then he either found him afterwards lying dead or somebody told him that the body had been found, and then he lost his head and bolted. Of course it doesn't very much matter now, because he is dead himself, poor old boy, and it's ten to one against the truth ever coming out; but that's my own firm conviction about it.'

Violet could not help thinking the theory a little far-fetched; but she liked Hubert all the better for entertaining it. 'At all events,' she remarked, 'Mr. Chaine can hardly object to your believing in your brother's innocence.'

'Oh, yes, he can—and what's more, he will. The governor is a queer sort of customer. He doesn't mean to be uncharitable;

but he won't allow anybody to differ from
him, and as he has made up his mind that
John was a murderer, he will be sure to get
into a thundering rage with me when I tell
him that that hasn't been proved yet. Well,
he'll have to rage, that's all; only I should
like to avoid putting up his back just now
if I could, because this coming home has
cost me a good bit of money, and a cheque
would be welcome.'

Hubert Chaine was one of those happy
men who retain some of the pleasantest
characteristics of boyhood up to an advanced
age. He always gave everybody credit for
being interested in what interested him; he
was never unwilling to talk in the most open
manner about himself and his private affairs;
and it is to be presumed that Violet did not
dislike that style of conversation, for she
walked about with him until after the next
race had been run, and when he had conducted her back to her chaperon's side, she
was glad to hear that good-natured lady
invite him to dine on the following evening.

'Hubert is far the best of that lot,' Lady Hartlepool remarked, on the way home. 'His family don't think much of him because he is supposed to have no brains to speak of; but at least he is a good, honest gentleman—and that is more than I should care to affirm about his clever brother Wilfrid. I wish he were a year older than Wilfrid !'

'Why should you wish to deprive him of such a large slice of life?' inquired Violet, laughing.

'Only because I should like him to be his father's heir,' answered Lady Hartlepool.

She was thinking that, if Hubert had been in that fortunate position, he would have made a much more suitable and desirable partner for Violet than Sir Harvey Amherst could be ; but of course she was not so foolish as to give utterance to her thoughts, and she had formed too high an opinion of Violet's common sense to fear lest anything untoward should result from the appearance of the good, honest gentleman at her dinner-table.

Still one cannot be too careful in one's

dealings with young people, very few of them being able, or even anxious, to resist the promptings of nature ; and if Lady Hartlepool was bound to show some hospitality to her cousin, it would doubtless have been wiser on her part to invite him for any evening rather than that on which she had been commanded to attend a State concert. For, as Miss Stanton had not had the honour of being included amongst Her Majesty's guests, and as she herself was obliged to go upstairs and change her gown immediately after dinner, while Lord Hartlepool was struggling into his lord-lieutenant's uniform, there was obviously nothing for it but to leave the two remaining members of the small party to entertain one another for three quarters of an hour.

It is superfluous to add that this was an arrangement which neither of the deserted ones felt to be in the least objectionable. Hubert ought, perhaps, to have gone away ; but he did not conceive it to be his duty to resign a chance of conversing with the girl whose image had been ever present to his mind's eye through so many long months, and as soon as they found themselves in undisturbed possession of the drawing-room he said :

'Suppose we go out upon the balcony? It's too hot and stuffy to sit indoors, and I dare say, if you wanted to be very kind, you would let me smoke a cigarette.'

Violet unhesitatingly accepted the suggestion and granted the request.   Between Lord Hartlepool's house and Park Lane there was a long strip of garden ; so that the broad balcony which adorned its façade combined the advantages of privacy and publicity. Sitting there upon a low easy-chair and gazing abstractedly at the flashing lamps of the carriages which passed to and fro before her in an unceasing double current, she was conscious of pausing for a while, as it were, to survey the ebb and flow of life, and the momentary respite was not unwelcome to her. Her companion's prattle, like the fragrance of his tobacco-smoke, produced a vaguely soothing impression upon her ; she did not hear a great deal of what he was saying and answered him, every now and then, somewhat at random, though it may very well be that her pleasant dreams would have been rudely dispelled by his departure.

To him, however, the scene and the situation presented themselves under another and a much more exciting aspect. He was a simple creature, as indeed the average young man (who differs so widely in that respect from the average young woman) usually is, and there really was not room in his mind at the time for more than one thought, namely, that he adored his neighbour. He was certainly aware that his means did not entitle him to contemplate marriage, and he would have admitted, in cold blood, that he had no business, under those circumstances, to make love to anybody; but these were matters of detail which he had no difficulty in dismissing from immediate consideration. Would it not, so far as that went, have been the most flagrant presumption on his part to imagine that there could

be any question of his love being returned?
He, therefore, with a light conscience, made
the most of his opportunity, and, to tell the
truth, he encountered no sort of discourage-
ment. Violet, as has been said before, liked
him; being a woman, she could not possibly
quarrel with any amount of liking that he
might have for her, and when he made so
bold as to assure her that his chief reason for
returning to England had been the prospect
of meeting her again, she neither disputed
nor seriously doubted the veracity of the
assertion. The youngest and most inex-
perienced of women soon acquire the conviction that no man's heart is in danger of
permanent injury from the accident of his
having fallen in love with them; and the
unfortunate part of it is that they are quite
right.

Nevertheless, the pangs of unrequited
love are sufficiently painful while they last,
and one would not wish any fellow-creature
to incur them if one could help it. Such,
at any rate, was the view taken by Lady

Hartlepool, who, when she appeared upon the balcony, arrayed in the family diamonds, overheard a few words which were not intended for any ear but Miss Stanton's.

'I'm afraid I must send you away now, Hubert,' said she. 'I'm sorry to appear so uncivil; but the carriage is waiting, and we are bound to be punctual to-night. Just come into the library for a minute before you go, though; I want to show you something.'

The young man rose obediently, with a sigh, and wished Miss Stanton good-night. 'We shall meet again soon,' said he; 'for I shall make a point of turning up at Anne's ball on Thursday.'

'That is all the more kind of you,' remarked his cousin, 'because I don't remember having sent you an invitation.'

'Well, you told me you were going to give a ball, anyhow,' returned Hubert, laughing; 'I'll excuse you for having neglected the proper formalities. And what have you brought me here to see?' he inquired, after

he had been conducted into the library and
the door had been closed.

'I forgot that there was no mirror in this
room,' answered Lady Hartlepool drily. 'If
there had been one, I could have shown you
the reflection of a goose. Come to us on
Thursday evening if you like, my dear boy,
and dance with Violet as often as she will
consent to dance with you; but don't go
and make a fool of yourself about her—it
isn't worth while. She is a very nice girl and
I like her very much, but she isn't quite so
unsophisticated as you probably imagine.
You may take my word for it that she will
never be guilty of the insanity of engaging
herself to a pauper. I must be off now—I
thought I would just warn you.'

Hubert did not care to deny that there
were grounds for the warning; he merely
remarked: 'I don't see how you can know so
much as all that about her, Anne.'

'Good gracious me!' returned Lady
Hartlepool impatiently, 'haven't I a pair of
eyes and a certain amount of intelligence?

Besides, I may as well tell you — because everybody knows it—that she is likely to become engaged before long to Sir Harvey Amherst.'

Hubert's jaw dropped. 'What! that old chap who was with her at Sandown?' he exclaimed. 'I didn't recognise him at the time, but I remembered him afterwards. Why, he was as old as he is now—or, at all events, he looked so—when I went to school!'

'Oh, well, of course. But there are no girls nowadays, and you are still, to all intents and purposes, a schoolboy; and as for Sir Harvey, he is a good sort of man in his way. I don't say that I should have chosen him for her; but she seems to have chosen him for herself, and, after all, I am not her mother. You must console yourself with the thought that you wouldn't be a bit better off if Sir Harvey Amherst were dead and buried.'

The consolation suggested did not commend itself favourably to Hubert, who made use of some forcible terms in denouncing the heartlessness of fashionable women and would have enlarged still further upon that theme, had he not been unceremoniously dismissed by his cousin.

'You must say all that some other time,' she interrupted; 'I literally haven't a moment more to spare now.'

So the lovelorn hussar was fain to leave the house and confide his sorrows to the stars, which winked down at him ironically, as they had been in the habit of doing upon countless forgotten generations of similar fools.

CHAPTER XXII

THE SORROWS OF HUBERT

There are two classes of mortals whose respective characters are almost invariably misconceived, namely, absolutely honest men and absolutely unscrupulous ones. And indeed this is but natural; because both are so very rare that few opportunities of observing them and their ways have ever been granted to the earnest student of human nature. Wilfrid Chaine, being simply devoid of any moral sense whatsoever, had from his youth up deceived nearly everybody with whom he had been brought into intimate relations; and although there were one or two persons, like Lady Hartlepool, who instinctively distrusted him, there were a great many more who believed firmly in his integrity. Amongst the latter no one was more conspicuous than his younger brother Hubert. That innocent and unsuspecting youth was wont to judge of people as he found them, and he had always found Wilfrid wise, kindly, and sympathetic. It was therefore no wonder that, at a time of some mental distress and perplexity, he should have felt irresistibly impelled to lay his case before so able and amiable a mentor.

Being, however, too shy to make an immediate confession of the fact that he had fallen hopelessly in love with Miss Violet Stanton, he only dropped in at Wilfrid's rooms one morning after breakfast and began to discourse upon a variety of topics, leading gradually up to his point with a good deal of superfluous circumlocution. After beating about the bush for the best part of half an hour, he remarked that he supposed he would have to go to Anne's ball on the following evening, and inquired, in a tone of elaborate unconcern which would not have misled an infant, whether Wilfrid knew any thing about that girl who was staying with her

—a daughter of some deceased Canon of St. Albyn's.

'I ask,' he was careful to explain, 'because I thought her rather a nice girl, and I was horrified to hear from Anne that there was a prospect of her engaging herself to old Amherst, who is looking out for a second wife, it seems. I hope it isn't true.'

'One always endeavours to hope that these things are not true,' answered Wilfrid with a scarcely perceptible smile; 'but one usually finds that they are. I also gathered from what Anne told me that she was doing her utmost to bring about this ill-assorted union, and I was as sorry as you are. Perhaps even a little more sorry; because I don't mind confessing to you in strict confidence that I myself had had some idea of entreating Miss Stanton to share my humble lot. Supposing that she thinks fit to refuse our friend Amherst, I may yet give her that chance of feathering her nest. I have had other things to think about lately, so that I have rather neglected her, I'm afraid; but if I can find

time, I'll try to go to Anne's ball and make
up my lee-way. Of course I can't pretend
to compete with Amherst in point of income;
but I have a few other advantages which he
can hardly boast of, and I ought in the course
of nature to be a tolerably rich man before
long. She might do better; but then again
she might do much worse.'

Consternation and disgust were vividly
depicted upon the younger man's countenance.
'I had no notion of this!' he exclaimed involuntarily. And then, in reproachful accents,
'You talk as though marriage were a mere
matter of bargain!'

'So it is, my dear boy. The upper, the
lower and the lower-middle classes, have
always regarded it in that light; it is only
that small section of the community known as
the upper-middle which marries for love, and
to the best of my knowledge and belief the
system does not work well in their case.
Miss Stanton nominally belongs to the upper-
middle; but she has the instincts of the upper
class, to which Anne has introduced her, and I

imagine that if she deigns to look favourably upon my suit, it will be because I have something substantial to offer her.'

'You really mean business, then?' asked Hubert dolefully.

'Well, yes; I think I may say that I do. My chief business just at present is to try and secure a seat in Parliament; but marriage has become a duty and a necessity for me now that poor John is dead, and upon the whole I would rather marry Miss Stanton than any other girl whom I know.'

After that, it was obviously out of the question to expect or solicit fraternal sympathy. Hubert dropped the subject, remarking airily that all this was no concern of his and that, for his own part, he trusted duty would never compel him to renounce the blessings of celibacy. Presently he took himself off to his club, where he sat for some little time in morose solitude, ruminating upon the depravity of the human race. He was not incensed against Wilfrid, whom he took to be a shrewd, but by no means evilly-disposed, man

of the world; he was only shocked to learn
that the sentiments which (as he well remembered) Violet had expressed with regard to
matrimony on the occasion of their first
meeting were those which she genuinely held
and was likely to act upon. He had fancied
her superior to the sordid considerations which
so many women profess, without quite meaning what they say; but that, doubtless, only
proved that he had been an ass. He resolved
that he would not trouble his head or his
heart any more about the girl. Let her marry
Sir Harvey or Wilfrid and be happy! It really
did not much matter which of them she might
see fit to take; although, for choice, he should
prefer not to have her for his sister-in-law.

Now, it might have been thought that, under
the circumstances, Hubert would scarcely have
cared to come all the way from Hounslow the
next evening for the purpose of attending
Lady Hartlepool's ball; but lovers are privileged to be inconsistent, and not a few disappointed lovers derive a certain bitter consolation
from proclaiming emphatically that they are

not disappointed at all. This, most probably, was the impression that Hubert intended to convey when he strolled into his cousin's ball-room and carelessly inquired of Miss Stanton whether she could give him a dance. If so, he might have spared himself the pains of acting a part with Violet, who at once noticed his altered manner and was not slow to divine its cause.

'Delighted,' she answered urbanely. 'Which will you have—the next one or number sixteen?'

Hubert said that, as he was afraid he would be obliged to leave before sunrise, he would take the next one, please; so for two or three minutes he had the enjoyment of waltzing with an admirable partner round one of the best ball-rooms in London. There was as yet no inconvenient crowd; the music was as good as the floor, and Violet danced beautifully; still he was willing enough to accede to her suggestion that they should sit out the remainder of the dance.

'I don't want to tire myself out in the

beginning of the evening,' she explained, by
way of apology, 'and I don't mind asking *you*
to stop, because you are too first-rate a per-
former to have unworthy suspicions and take
offence at them.'

He thanked her for the compliment and
assured her that he had no suspicions of the
kind to which she alluded. He had, however,
other suspicions of a far more serious de-
scription; and these her behaviour, after they
had seated themselves in a corner, tended
unhappily to confirm. For at first she refused
altogether to see the point of his ironical
remarks about the sacrifices which young
women in general are ready to make for the
sake of mere wealth, and then, perceiving that
he was not to be diverted from his purpose,
she took him aback by saying calmly:

'I suppose you wouldn't abuse us all round
in this way unless you meant your abuse to
apply particularly to me. Perhaps Lady
Hartlepool has been telling you that I am less
sentimental and have a keener eye to business
than is becoming at my age? Well, that may

be true; but at least no one can accuse me of having pretended to be anything except what I am. I have always acknowledged that I am not sentimental and that I can't see why it shouldn't be just as much a girl's duty as a man's to get hold of money, if she can.'

'But it isn't a man's duty to get hold of money except by some trade or profession,' objected the young moralist whom she addressed; 'he isn't exactly admired for making it in any other way.'

'He would be if there were no trades or professions open to him—which happens, you see, to be our sad case. A girl, if she is very lucky, may get the chance of marrying a rich man and, if she is superlatively lucky, she may adore him into the bargain; but it really doesn't do to expect superlatives. Personally, I should be quite satisfied with such a positive blessing as £20,000 a year, or even half as much. An aged and hideous bridegroom would be a drawback, no doubt; but I should never dream of allowing myself to be scared by it.'

This little bit of self-portraiture was somewhat too highly coloured to be accepted as sincere; but the ingenuous Hubert took it quite literally and looked very sombre over it.

'Well, Miss Stanton,' he remarked, 'I could understand an ill-natured person saying that sort of thing about you; but upon my word, I can't understand your saying it about yourself.'

'Can't you?' returned Violet, with a slight accession of colour. 'Well—perhaps it doesn't so very much signify even if you can't.'

He perceived that he had very nearly succeeded in making her lose her temper; but, as he had not aspired to the achievement of that small triumph, he was in no way elated or consoled by it. 'One of these days you will find out that you have made a very great mistake,' was the only rejoinder which suggested itself to him.

'That,' observed Violet, recovering herself and laughing, 'is precisely what my mother and every experienced person whom I have ever met would tell me if I were to take it into my head to marry a poor curate. I

haven't the slightest doubt that they would be
right; so I shall endeavour to steel my heart
against poor curates.'

'And against poor subalterns, I presume?'

'Naturally. How fortunate it is for me
that subalterns can hardly be described as
irresistible by their best friends! I forget
whether you are a subaltern or not; but I
dare say you will excuse my saying that, after
having seen a good deal of them at St. Albyn's,
I have come to the conclusion that a more
densely stupid class of mortals doesn't exist.'

'Please accept my warmest thanks and
acknowledgments on behalf of myself and
the service generally,' answered Hubert, who
was now growing angry in his turn. 'Very
likely we are most of us stupid; but I am not
sure that it isn't better to be stupid than to
be too clever by half.'

Sir Harvey Amherst, very smart and
sprightly in knee-breeches and black silk
stockings, appeared upon the scene just in
time to avert an undignified altercation. He
had been dining with a royal personage, it

seemed, and had therefore been unable to present himself earlier. He trusted, however, that Miss Stanton had not forgotten to reserve the dances which she had so kindly promised him. Having been informed, with somewhat exaggerated emphasis, that Miss Stanton never forgot pleasant engagements, he turned to the young man who was scowling at him over her fan and affably introduced himself.

'I am glad to hear that your father is a little better,' said he. 'I used often to meet him when he was in the House; but we have lost sight of one another latterly. Please give him my kind remembrances when you see him.'

Hubert grunted out 'All right,' and was rude enough to add, 'I suppose you were at school with the governor, weren't you?'

'Well, no,' answered Sir Harvey good-humouredly; 'I can't claim to have had that honour. Ancient as I am, I did play in the Eton eleven against Harrow within living memory.'

The merciless Hubert was upon the point

of inquiring in what year Sir Harvey had formed one of the Eton eleven; but Violet whispered a word or two to her elderly admirer, who at once offered her his arm and led her away; so that insulting query remained un-uttered.

It now only remained for a thoroughly disenchanted and disgusted young officer to shake the dust of Lady Hartlepool's ballroom off the soles of his shoes and return to barracks. Upon the staircase he encountered Wilfrid, who laughed and said, 'Had enough of it already?'

'More than enough,' he answered curtly; 'this sort of thing is poor fun for outsiders. You're here on business, I suppose? Well, you had better look sharp if you don't want to be cut out by that made-up old rival of yours. He was skipping round the room with Miss Stanton just now as if he had never heard of such a thing as gout in his life.'

Now, if in the whole range of human experience there is one thing more absolutely certain and more commonly disputed than another, it is that the malady known as falling

in love is a transient affliction ; and a very
great comfort this reflection ought to be to
those who have had the ill luck to set their
affections upon an unworthy object.   As a
rule, however, they do not seem anxious to be
comforted or grateful to the friends who do
their best to comfort them.   Nobody was so
officious as to comfort Hubert, because nobody
knew what was the matter with him ; but his
brother officers found him uncommonly poor
company at this time, while he, on his side,
was so little amused by the horse-play which
had once delighted him that he was fain to
ask leave for a few days and run down to
Southshire to visit his parents.

But if there was no bear-fighting at Chaine
Court, neither was any amusement or comfort
obtainable there.   As he had anticipated, he
fell out with his father upon the subject of the
family disgrace and, after a lengthy discussion,
was ordered to be silent in that fine old per-
emptory style with which Mr. Chaine's children
had always had reason to be familiar.   As for
his mother, she very soon wormed his secret

out of him, though he did not go the length of avowing it in so many words ; after which she was heartless enough to laugh at him.

'I remember that you were smitten with my friend Violet the first time that you met her,' she remarked. 'Didn't you give her a lead over a five-barred gate, or something ? So you have really been constant to her all this long time ! How funny of you !'

'I never gave her a lead over a five-barred gate, as it happens,' answered Hubert crossly, 'and I never said that I had been smitten with her or that I had remained constant to her. Although, if you come to that, I can't for the life of me see what there would be so very funny in my having done all those things.'

'Oh, constancy is always rather funny,' returned Lady Elizabeth. 'Anyhow, it is rather strange, and not what one expects of a boy of your age, who will have to pass through a great many flirtations before he can take the liberty of falling seriously in love with anybody. Now Wilfrid is really

a serious person, besides being of an age to
marry and having the means to do it.   I
should be glad if he were serious about Violet
Stanton, because she is a nice girl and I think
she would suit him very well.   Still, of course,
his choice isn't restricted to her; and if, as
you seem to imagine, she prefers Sir Harvey
Amherst—well, it can't be helped.   All I
have to say about it is that I wonder at her
taste.'

Hubert observed that old Amherst was
rather more of a catch than Wilfrid, he
supposed, but that he really didn't care
which of the rivals Miss Stanton was likely
to favour.   He did, indeed, try very hard to
persuade himself that he didn't care what
became of her; but not succeeding in this
endeavour, and finding his parents neither
sympathetic nor particularly anxious to retain
him with them, he cut his visit shorter than
he had intended to do.

For the same sufficient or insufficient
reasons he decided to stop a night in London
before rejoining his regiment, and, having

arrayed himself in his very best clothes,
made for his cousin's house in Park Lane
between five and six o'clock on the afternoon
of his arrival.

One should never, even in the case of near
relations, neglect those civilities which politeness requires, and after having been present
at a ball it is certainly right to leave cards
upon one's entertainers. It was not, to be
sure, Hubert's original design to confine himself to that formal ceremony ; but it became
so when he reached his destination, where a
rather disagreeable surprise awaited him.
For no sooner had he dismissed his hansom
than a very smart coach was pulled up at
the door, and upon the box sat Sir Harvey
Amherst, with Violet Stanton by his side,
while behind them were Lord and Lady
Hartlepool, together with sundry young men
and maidens unknown to the disgusted
spectator.

Well, after witnessing such a truly revolt-
ing sight as that (because of course Miss
Stanton's appearance on the box-seat of Sir

Harvey's drag was nothing more nor less than
an ostentatious advertisement of her engagement), it seemed best to ring the bell hastily,
push two cards into the letter-box and bolt;
but poor Hubert had been seen by his cousins,
who intercepted him as he was turning away
and hospitably insisted upon refreshing him
with a cup of tea. He had to submit, therefore, to what could not very well be avoided
without an appearance of displeasure which
might seem slightly ridiculous, and Lady
Hartlepool, who took him under her wing,
making him sit beside her while she poured
out the tea, evidently felt more sorry for
him than some nearer relatives of his had
been.

'Oh, I suppose so,' she said, with a touch
of impatience in answer to the question which
he could not resist putting. 'Nothing has
been said to me as yet; but it certainly looks
as if the girl had made up her mind; and,
after all, she may be right, you know. Life
isn't a romantic business, though middle-aged
people and very young ones are fond of

making believe that it is. I am middle-aged
and you are very young, so that we naturally
like to make believe as much as we can; but
the chances are that, if we could have our
own way with the world, we should create all
manner of bothers and unpleasantnesses. Let
us be thankful that that responsibility is off
our hands. To-morrow I shall be relieved of
all responsibility for Miss Violet, who is going
home to her mother.'

'For the purpose of announcing that she
has promised to marry that venerable cari-
cature of a masher, I presume?' said Hubert
gloomily.

Lady Hartlepool jerked up her shoulders.
'Very likely; but, as I tell you, I haven't
had the honour of being admitted into her
confidence. Personally, I must acknowledge
that I have nothing to complain of, and that
if she becomes Lady Amherst she will bring
credit upon herself and upon me. Introducing
any girl who isn't one's own daughter to
society is always a hazardous undertaking,
and I ought to be very thankful to her for

having given me so little anxiety.   Suppose
she had taken a fancy to some unmarriageable
young fellow, such as yourself, for example—
a nice mess I should have been in !   And, as
far as that goes, a nice mess he would have
been in too !   No, my dear Hubert, you may
depend upon it that whatever is is right, and
that we none of us know what is best for us.
Now perhaps, since you are here, you will be
kind enough to attend to your immediate
duties and hand round the cakes and bread-
and-butter.'

It was a very sullen and taciturn young
man who performed that duty, and little
reward did any of the ladies present meet
with in return for the kindly smiles with
which they acknowledged his attention.   So
far as he was concerned, there was only one
lady present ; and he did not give her a
chance of smiling upon him, because she had
chosen to retire to the extreme end of the
room with Sir Harvey Amherst, who, it
might be assumed, was capable of ministering
to her wants.   Sir Harvey, with his elbows

on his knees and his back turned towards the company, was talking to her with much apparent earnestness, and no doubt he would have been greatly annoyed by any interruption at that particular moment.

'I can quite enter into your feelings, Miss Stanton,' he was saying. 'You must have known for some time past what mine have been; still, I daresay, I have spoken rather sooner than you expected, and I don't wonder at your wanting a little time for consideration. As for me, I can only say that I am too grateful to you for not having rejected me outright to be impatient. In a few weeks I hope to be down in the country, and then, with your permission, I will call upon you at St. Albyn's and beg for your final answer. Is that a bargain?'

Violet was not looking at him; she was gazing abstractedly at the group round Lady Hartlepool's tea-table, in which a prominent figure was that of a former friend of hers who had not so much as deigned to shake hands with her.

'Yes,' she replied at length, 'that shall be the bargain. The whole thing will be a bargain, won't it?—that is, if I consent to it. I hope you clearly understand that I look at the matter in that way. We have been very good friends; but of course I am not in love with you, and I don't for a moment pretend that I should accept you if you were poor.'

Sir Harvey pulled a rather wry face, for he did not much like that 'of course.' However, he gallantly concealed any mortification that he may have felt and declared that Miss Stanton's candour only increased his admiration and respect for her. 'And perhaps I may venture to add,' he continued, 'that I don't altogether despair of eventually earning the love which you refuse me just now, since I have your word for it that no one else has been more fortunate than I in that respect.'

'Oh, there is no one else,' answered Violet unhesitatingly. 'I don't think I am at all a susceptible sort of person; susceptibility isn't in my line.'

Sir Harvey glanced at her with a half-amused, whimsical sort of smile. He had seen a good deal of women in his time, and he thought he knew enough about them to be pretty sure that Miss Stanton was not so hard-hearted as she made herself out. He was much too old to be at all foolishly in love; but naturally he did not take that view of himself, nor perhaps was it unnatural that he should have been blind to the absurdity of imagining that a girl might fall in love with him. He had been told as distinctly as possible that, if he obtained what he wished for, it would be only because he was a rich man; but, having been a rich man for close upon half a century, he was aware of the supreme importance of wealth as a factor in all human affairs, so that this avowal did not shock or discourage him. He considered command of money to be one of his recommendations and fully expected it to be taken into account, together with good birth, good looks and good manners.

In any case, he felt no sort of fear of the

young soldier at the opposite end of the room, who was at that moment taking leave of Lady Hartlepool, and who apparently did not deem it incumbent upon him to pay a similar compliment to Miss Stanton.

CHAPTER XXIII

A FRIEND OF IDA'S RETURNS

THE Very Reverend the Dean of St. Albyn's, being a man who prided himself upon a punctilious observance of all the duties which belonged to his position, rarely failed to put in an appearance at the cathedral services, though in his heart of hearts he would often have been glad to shirk them. One afternoon he had divested himself of his surplice, as usual, had—also as usual—addressed a few urbane words to the officiating minor canon and was stepping slowly homewards when he was overtaken by Canon Mayne, who was then in residence. Canon Mayne, a timid old gentleman, with sparse sandy hair, round shoulders and a shuffling gait, did not, as a rule, speak to anybody unless he was spoken to or had something particular to say. The

Dean, therefore, naturally paused, on being accosted, and looked down at him with a benevolent, reassuring smile.

'Anything you wish to consult me about, Mayne?' he inquired.

'Oh no, nothing—nothing at all, thank you,' answered the other hurriedly. 'I saw you in front of me, and I thought, as we were going the same way——'

He paused, gave a nervous little giggle, dropped his umbrella, picked it up again and, receiving no assistance from his ecclesiastical superior, resumed: 'Beautiful weather, is it not? So glad that there is some prospect of a good harvest at last.'

'I understand that the yield is likely to be below the average,' returned the Dean, who presumed that Canon Mayne had not intruded upon his privacy for the purpose of discussing the weather and the crops. 'Fortunately, the depression in the value of land no longer affects us as a body.'

'True—true; we may congratulate our-selves upon having arranged matters with the

Ecclesiastical Commissioners in more prosperous times ; still, for the sake of the farmers,
one is pleased to see the sun shining,' Canon
Mayne observed.

He shuffled along for another fifty yards
or so in silence ; after which he sighed
(having evidently abandoned as impractic-
able any attempt to lead up to his point by
degrees) and said abruptly :

'Arthur came home last night.'

'Ah, indeed ?' answered the Dean, understanding what was meant by this announcement, but not caring to admit that it possessed
any personal interest for him. 'It must be
pleasant for you and Mrs. Mayne to have your
son with you once more. He is doing well in
his profession, I trust.'

'Wonderfully well, I am thankful to say,
considering how short a time he has been
practising. He has been quite busy of late ;
but just now, you know, the Courts have risen
for the long vacation.'

'Which he proposes to spend at home, I
hope,' the Dean said amiably. 'Pray re-

member me to him, and tell him that I shall
always be glad to see him, if he thinks it
worth while to call at the Deanery.'

Canon Mayne looked greatly relieved.
'Thank you very much,' he replied; 'I will
not fail to deliver your kind message, which
will be most welcome to Arthur, I am sure.
He was saying this morning that he would
like to pay a round of visits to his friends
here and—and hereabouts.'

The Dean inclined his head graciously and
changed the subject.   He appeared to have
forgotten certain episodes in the past career of
this rising young barrister; but his memory
was not really so short, nor, when he reached
home, did his countenance any longer wear an
expression of benignity.   Indeed, since there
was nobody to hear him, he went the length
of ejaculating, 'Bother the fellow!   I wonder
whether he has come down here on purpose
to give me trouble again.'

It did not, upon reflection, seem by any
means improbable that he had; moreover,
there was a very fair chance indeed of his

succeeding in his nefarious design. Decency, no doubt, ought to prevent, and perhaps would prevent, Ida from renewing relations with him in these early days of her widowhood ; but Ida was not altogether to be depended upon, and it was at least conceivable that she might be foolish and selfish enough to contract a second marriage which her father was hardly in a position to forbid. This was a very grievous thought ; because it could not be supposed that old Mr. Chaine's liberality to his son's widow would be continued in the event of her becoming the wife of another man.

Under these circumstances there could be little room for doubt as to the duty of paying a paternal visit to the White House, whither the good Dean accordingly bent his steps on the ensuing afternoon. His daughter received him and his platitudes in her customary spirit, which was not quite all that a fond parent could have desired it to be ; but the Dean was very forbearing. Not until he had sat with her for a good half hour did he remark casually :

'I hate discussions about money matters ; still it is both wrong and foolish to neglect such things, and I confess, my dear child, that I sometimes feel a little anxious about your future. Is it the case that Mr. Chaine has made any absolute settlement upon you, or do you depend for your means of subsistence entirely upon his good will and pleasure ? '

'He makes me the allowance that you know of,' answered Ida, 'and he has promised to provide for me in his will. I don't think you have any reason to feel anxious about me.'

The Dean shook his head. ' Promises,' said he, 'are seldom unconditional, and I have known instances of their having been broken even when they have appeared to be so. As far as I am able to judge of Mr. Chaine's character, I should doubt whether you could safely cross him in any way ; nor indeed could he fairly be blamed for casting you adrift in the event of your acting in such a manner as to displease him. I think, my dear, that, without being at all worldly or greedy, you would do well always to bear in mind that your prospects are essentially precarious.'

'I will bear it in mind,' answered Ida. 'Perhaps you have some particular reason for giving me this caution?'

The Dean disclaimed particular reasons; but, as he had no wish to conceal the fact that such reasons existed, he proceeded at once to mention Arthur Mayne's return to the neighbourhood. 'Not,' he hastened to add, 'that you are at all likely to meet the young man, for you are so seldom in St. Albyn's, and of course he will understand that you do not care to admit visitors just now; still I thought it best to prepare you for the possibility of your encountering him by chance. An encounter of that kind might be awkward, you know, considering what took place prior to his departure, and I am sure you would prefer to avoid it.'

He had fully expected to be told that she did not see why such an encounter should be awkward, and that she had no desire to shrink from it; her reply, therefore, came upon him as an agreeable surprise. 'I would certainly rather not see him,' she said hurriedly. 'I suppose, as you say, he isn't very likely to call here; but if you could manage to give his father a hint that I don't receive visits at present, I should be glad.'

The Dean undertook to perform this commission discreetly, and went away comforted. Bygone events had justified him in regarding his daughter as a wilful and wayward woman; but he now perceived, with great thankfulness, that she had sense enough to know on which side her bread was buttered. It is superfluous to add that he did not put things in so coarse and vulgar a way; only that was what he really meant when, on saying his prayers before going to bed, he expressed his gratitude to Heaven for having blessed him with a good and wise child.

He would have been by no means so sure that he possessed that blessing, had he been capable of drawing the most ordinary deductions from feminine utterances. The reader, who is doubtless aware that women seldom or never mean what they say, will have surmised that Ida was, above all things, anxious to set eyes once more upon the only man whom she had ever loved, and will not be surprised to hear that she honestly believed herself anxious to keep out of his way. That his love for her must have been killed by her marriage she could not doubt; that he might conceive it to be his duty to pay her a visit of commiseration was not improbable; and that it would be extremely painful and humiliating to be pitied by him was the strongest sentiment of which she was conscious. Consequently, for a week after she had received the news from her father, she took care to be out every afternoon, as well as to shun frequented paths, and why she should have returned home each evening with a feeling of bitter disappointment she really did not know.

However, she could not carry self-deception quite so far as to repress a sudden leaping up of the heart when at length she was brought face to face with one whom she had done her very best to elude. It was no fault of hers that she came across Mr. Mayne one evening in a narrow lane, whence escape was impossible; and he must have been eager to convince her that it was also no fault of his, for he had no sooner shaken hands with her than he made haste to explain that he had only strolled out from St. Albyn's for a country walk.

'I should have paid my respects to you before this,' he added quite composedly; 'but the Dean told my father, who told me, that you did not wish to be bothered.'

Ida corrected him with frigid politeness. It was not a bother to her to see her acquaintances every now and then; but it must, of course, be a bother to them to come all the way out from St. Albyn's upon the chance of finding her at home; and as she had occupations in the neighbourhood which filled up nearly the whole of her spare time, she had thought it best to intimate to those at a distance that they might regard themselves as released from conventional courtesies so far as she was concerned.

Arthur Mayne replied that he could quite understand that; yet, instead of accepting his dismissal, he turned round and walked down the lane beside her. He was not at all embarrassed; he talked easily and fluently about subjects in which neither he nor his hearer were interested; as far as could be gathered, he wished to convey the impression that he was content to let bygones be bygones. This attitude of his was naturally a great relief to Ida, and, lest he should make any mistake about the matter, she took some pains to let him see that she regarded it as such. If he had forgotten certain youthful follies and differences, so much the better. She herself had not forgotten them, because she happened to have a retentive memory; but it was, of course, an immense comfort to her to know that she might now, without risk of possible misconception, associate on friendly terms with one for whom she had always felt a sincere regard. This, or something equivalent to this, was what she was careful to explain to him while they paced, side by side, between the

high banks and under the overarching trees.
She was also kind enough to make inquiries
as to his progress in his profession, and to
express her heartfelt satisfaction on being
informed that he was really getting on re-
markably well. However, she cut him rather
short when he, on his side, began to put a few
tentative questions.

'Oh, there is nothing to be said about me,'
she answered; 'I am like those happy nations
whose history can't be written. I eat, drink
and sleep, and I have no troubles—which is
delightful. Now I must say good-bye. If
you walk back about a hundred yards and
take the first turn to the left, you will hit off
a footpath which will take you straight to St.
Albyn's.'

'I believe I am to be dragged to an afternoon entertainment at Hatton Park next
Thursday,' Arthur Mayne observed, as a sort
of afterthought, on taking leave of her.
'Might I call, upon the chance of finding
you at home, when I am released?'

'Pray don't trouble to go through that

ceremony,' Ida replied; 'it really isn't necessary, and I'm afraid I can't promise to be in
at any given hour. I will take the will for
the deed.'

Nevertheless, she did chance to be at home
when Mr. Mayne rang her door-bell on the
day mentioned, and it is not unfair to assume
that she would have been a good deal annoyed
if he had failed to keep his promise. In the·
interim she had searched her heart and conscience to such good purpose that she was
able to receive him as an old and valued
friend ought to be received. The past was
dead and buried—he was evidently sensible
enough or fickle enough to recognise that—
while, for her own part, she rejoiced to think
that the romance of her girlhood had come to
an end without serious prejudice to anybody's
happiness.

'I am in luck,' he remarked, with a pleasant
smile, as he took possession of the chair which
she pushed forward for him. 'I had so little
hope of seeing you to-day that I was driven,
as the next best thing, to talk about you to

the Miss Frasers, who couldn't find words to
praise you highly enough.   They tell me that
you are a sort of good fairy to the poor and
the sick, and that the parish would go to wrack
and ruin if you ever left it.'

'I believe it got on tolerably well before I
came here,' answered Ida, 'and it will probably
survive my death.   The poor and the sick are
more indebted to the Fraser girls than they
are to me ; still I manage to help a little, and,
such as my help is, they may count upon
having it as long as I live.'

Such, in truth, was her expectation and
intention.   After the calamities which had
befallen her, there could be nothing except a
solitary existence to look forward to, nor anything to hope for beyond peace and quietness
and the opportunity of alleviating some of the
misfortunes of others.   She was not discontented ; but she felt rather old—a great deal
older, for example, than Arthur Mayne, who
had the world before him and a fine provision
of health and talent wherewith to conquer the
same.   In talking to him she was pleased to

adopt a quasi-maternal tone; she took it for granted that his whole heart was in his profession, that he was bent upon success and likely to achieve it; and if her manner was a shade more patronising than he liked, he did not intimate that it was so.

He behaved, in short, very well indeed—almost too well. Not the most remote allusion to either of the two dead men, whom he might have been pardoned for regarding as personal enemies, escaped him; never a word did he say which could be construed as expressing compassion for the forlorn state of the woman whom he had once loved; the Dean of St. Albyn's might have heard the whole of his conversation and would only have been reassured by it. This being so, there was no need whatsoever to snub him when, on taking his leave, he begged permission to repeat his visit.

'I shall always be glad to see you if you are out this way and inclined to look me up,' was Ida's reply to this modest request; 'only, as I told you before, I can't undertake to say that

I shall be in the house at any time between luncheon and dinner. I have a good many jobs of one kind and another to attend to, and so, I suppose, have you, though this is the holiday season.'

He did not contradict her, and did not call again for a week, during which time—as was only natural—she thought about him a great deal. He had changed; in some respects, doubtless, he had improved; he was better looking and better mannered than of yore, and she appreciated the delicacy which had restrained him from referring to her domestic sorrows. Still the fact remained that he had changed; and that, after all, is almost the worst offence of which one's friends can possibly be guilty.

'To be sure, I have changed also,' reflected Ida, by way of excusing him. 'We all change as time goes on, and we can't help it, and I suppose it is just as well that we do. All the same, it seems strange that I should so completely have misread his character.'

It would have been still more strange if she

had interpreted his character correctly ; for he
was not quite the sort of man whom one meets
every day.   The affections of the everyday
sort of man can hardly be expected to survive
such a shock as his had sustained by Ida's
marriage ; nor, even when they do so, are they
likely to be held in check by common sense
and self-control.   But Arthur Mayne was one
of those quiet, steadfast fellows who very
often secure what they want in the long run.
He had done his best to forget the woman
whom he loved ; but, as he had not succeeded,
his hopes had naturally revived when he had
heard that she was once more free ; and he was
not such a fool as to ruin those hopes by precipitate action.   His best chance, he was wise
enough to perceive, lay in gradually accustom-
ing her to his society : it would have been
sheer insanity to begin making love to her
within a few months of John Chaine's tragic
disappearance and death.

Reasoning thus, he absented himself from
the White House for a whole week, and when
he did return thither, was as sober and com-

monplace in his conversation as Mrs. John
Chaine's best friends could have desired him
to be. It was Ida who, after a time, grew
impatient of a reticence which ought not to
exist between friends and who alluded of her
own accord to the terrible events which had
wrecked her life.

'You talk as though I were like the rest of
the world,' she said abruptly to her visitor one
afternoon. 'It is kind of you to ignore the
truth, and I am not ungrateful; but the truth,
of course, is that, though I am not exactly to
blame for what has happened, I shall have to
suffer for it to my dying day, and that most
people will always think me a little to blame
for it.'

'I am quite sure that you were not in the
least to blame,' Arthur Mayne affirmed emphatically.

'That is absurd—how can you know? In
reality I was just so far to blame that when I
saw that my husband was jealous without a
cause, I didn't trouble myself to reassure him.
What he did was what I never for a moment

imagined that he would dream of doing; still that is a poor excuse, and the punishment that has come upon me has been well deserved.'

'What punishment?' the young barrister made so bold as to inquire.

'Ah! I understand what you mean; and the misfortune is that you are quite right. I was glad and thankful to hear of his death; I am living upon his money—or at least upon the money which would have been his—and I am delivered from a man who had become hateful to me. No wonder you ask what punishment I have to complain of! Yet, if you will think a little longer, you will realise perhaps that the ordinary allowance of self-respect might be worth rather more to me than all the material comforts that I enjoy.'

She spoke with unwonted warmth, and indeed meant every word that she said. Arthur Mayne, on his side, had much ado to keep himself from saying all that he meant: nevertheless, he managed to accomplish this and to be discreet as well as sympathetic. However, he did feel that the seal of silence had now been removed from his lips, and after the above colloquy his style of conversation with Ida became, as may well be imagined, at once more interesting and less disinterested.

Fortunately, the Dean of St. Albyn's, upon whom he did not deem it necessary to call, was unaware that he was in the habit of going out for long afternoon walks and that these were invariably shaped towards the same point of the compass.

CHAPTER XXIV

ANOTHER FRIEND DEPARTS

It is possible to be a dean and to have written learned treatises and at the same time to be rather a fool. This assertion, many people will be unkind enough to say, stands in no need of being supported by examples; yet, for the benefit of those who fondly imagine that a dignitary of the Church must of necessity be a sage, it may be regretfully mentioned here that Dean Pemberton was not quite as wise as he looked. Had he been so, he would scarcely have flattered himself that the caution which he had addressed to his daughter, and her satisfactory reply thereto, sufficed to relieve him of all anxiety with regard to Arthur Mayne, nor, when Ida casually informed him that that young man had called upon her more than once, would he have jumped to the conclusion that there could be no danger in visits so calmly and candidly confessed.

As a matter of fact, there was (from the Dean's point of view) considerable danger in them; but of this it is only fair to state that Ida herself was perfectly unconscious. She was not, perhaps, at all hours of the day and night unconscious of the fact that her heart remained, as it always had remained, true to her first and only love; still she pretty generally contrived to persuade herself that she had changed almost as much as he had and that she was thankful to possess in him a friend who no longer wished to be anything more than her friend. If he had wished for anything more, he could not have had it— that was certain. Her punishment (as she had intended to imply when mentioning it to him) consisted in her being the widow of a murderer who might have been alive and prosperous and innocent of crime but for her. It was obvious that a woman thus afflicted must bear her burden alone, and that, whatever her future fate might be, it could not be other than a solitary one.

It was all the more likely to be so, because Arthur Mayne's avocations must, of course, soon take him away, because she did not make friends easily and because there really was no one in the neighbourhood whom she cared very much to see, unless indeed it might be her father-in-law. Between her and the old gentleman there had of late sprung up an intimacy which was perhaps due to some unexpressed community of sentiment — to a remorseful consciousness that one who had never been dear to either of them had met with little mercy at their hands. When Mr. Chaine came down to the White House alone, as he sometimes did, and sat for a while with Ida, he avoided mentioning John's name ; but every now and then he would make distant allusions which she was able to interpret and to which, in the same vague fashion, she would respond. It would have been almost impossible for a man of his nature to admit, even to himself, that he had ever been guilty of injustice; but he was saddened by occasional memories of the unvarying harshness with which he had treated the son who was dead and gone, and probably he had some comforting sense of making reparation to him, as well as to his widow, by those visits and those half-confidences. That he owed reparation to Ida he did not mind saying openly; because, for one thing, it was more his misfortune than his fault that such should be the case, and, for another, he had dealt with her as handsomely and liberally as he knew how. He had not told her, nor could she possibly ask him, the precise arrangements that he had made on her behalf; but she had been given to understand that the White House would be hers for life. This provision, no doubt, would be made subject to the customary conditions: Ida was quite of one mind with the Dean in assuming that re-marriage on her part would necessarily cancel it. That, however, was of no consequence, since a second marriage appeared to her as utterly out of the question as she was sure it must appear to the testator.

Now it came to pass, one afternoon, that old Mr. Chaine, who had been sitting beside her in silence for some little time, suddenly made a speech which astonished her beyond measure.

'My dear,' said he, 'you are a young woman, you are in excellent health, and humanly speaking you may expect to be in this world twice as long as you have already lived. Looking forward into the future, I cannot but recognise the probability of your marrying again, and I think I ought to tell you before I die that, in my opinion, you would do well and wisely to form fresh ties and interests for yourself. It seems to me that a woman who has neither husband nor children is almost as badly off as a man who has no profession.'

'I don't feel like that about it,' answered Ida, colouring a little; 'my life is practically over—at all events my youth is—and it would not be possible for me to make a fresh start. One can't obliterate the past.'

'That would naturally be your present

feeling; but a few years hence you will find that the past is growing dim, and what I wish you to understand is that, so far as I can make you free, you will be free to form new plans for the future. I mean that the money which I have bequeathed to you will be yours absolutely to do what you like with. This house will only be yours during the term of your widowhood, because I did not think it fair to my successors to leave any part of the property away from them permanently; but your legacy will not be much larger than what you would have been entitled to expect under your husband's will, so that you need not feel any scruple about accepting it. It should bring you in £1500 a year, or thereabouts. You will think me unfeeling, I am afraid, for using such plain language upon a subject which can hardly have entered into your thoughts as yet: my excuse is that I may not have another opportunity of doing so and that I am anxious to spare you misgivings which might have troubled you later if I had held my peace.'

'You are very good to me,' said Ida gratefully; for she was touched by the old man's kindness, though it did not in any degree modify her own determination.

'No,' he answered; 'I have done no more for you than it was my duty to do. I wish I could be sure that I had done my duty also to others! I have tried to do right; but in these last days of my life I sometimes doubt and fear —Well, all things will soon be made clear to me; for I have very nearly done with this present world. Did it ever occur to you, Ida, to wonder what will happen to us all the moment after death?'

'Oh yes; I suppose that has occurred to everybody,' Ida replied.

'One would think so; yet in reality few people care to speculate upon the unknown and the unknowable. For my own part, I have been content to perform what appeared to be my daily duties and to leave the future to my Creator; still, now that I am upon the very brink of eternity, I find myself a little uneasy and bewildered. The Popish doctrine of purgatory would explain away many difficulties; but there is no warrant for it—no Scriptural warrant whatsoever.'

She divined that he was thinking of his son rather than of himself, and, to comfort him, she said, 'We can't tell who are sinners and who are not. All sorts of crimes which seem unpardonable to us may not really be worse than our own little ordinary shortcomings.'

He bent his head, smiling faintly. 'That may well be so,' he answered. 'Let us forgive and forget, then, as we hope that our sins also may be forgiven and forgotten.'

The sentiment, or rather the manner of its expression, was in curious contrast with the rules in accordance with which this stern moralist had lived; but indeed he was not at all like himself that day, and when Ida took his arm presently to help him out to his carriage, she could not help asking him whether he was feeling ill.

'Not so much ill, my dear, as dying,' he replied. 'I couldn't explain exactly what my sensations are; only for the last week or more I have known that my end was at hand. The doctor came to see me yesterday, and I am sure that he knows it too, though he assured Lady Elizabeth that there was nothing the matter. I am glad to have had this little talk with you. Don't forget what I have said, and don't let any one persuade you, when the time comes, that I didn't mean it all.'

At a later period these farewell words of Mr. Chaine's recurred to Ida's memory and caused her to wonder whether he had not possessed a somewhat clearer insight into the character of his heir than he had cared to avow; but for the moment she paid little heed to them. What her mind was full of, as she turned back into the house, was the old man's generosity and consideration for her. He had had no particular reason to love her; he might even have been justified in harbouring a grudge against her; yet he had been, upon the whole, the best friend that she had ever had, and tears came into her eyes at the thought that she was about to lose him.

For, notwithstanding the wonderful rally that he had made, and the doctor's assertion that there was nothing the matter with him, Mr. Chaine was evidently within sight of death. Even before he had mentioned his own presentiment, Ida had been struck by the mental and physical change which had come over him, and it was therefore no surprise to her when she was summoned to Chaine Court on the following day by a groom who had ridden over in hot haste to announce that the Squire had been taken seriously ill.

'I couldn't rightly say what 'tis, m'm,' was the man's reply to her inquiry, 'but I did hear tell as 'twas some sort o' seizure. Mr. Wilfrid was telegraphed for last night, and come down by the first train this mornin'. 'Tis a bad job, m'm, I'm afeared.'

Well, all depends upon what may be considered to be a bad job. Such of us as possess singing voices are wont to sigh for the Heavenly Jerusalem on most Sundays of the year when we lend our valuable aid to the choir in a musical rendering of those astonishing poetical compositions known as hymns, and the death of an old and careworn man ought not, one would think, to be regarded precisely in the light of a calamity; yet it may very well be that Mr. Chaine (who firmly believed himself destined to reach an abode of eternal happiness) was in no greater hurry than other people to set out for those undiscovered scenes. At all events, he had to undertake the quest, as we all must sooner or later, and perhaps it was no bad thing for him or for those about him that he was likely to enter upon it in a state of unconsciousness. When Ida arrived at Chaine Court she was met by Wilfrid, who had assumed a demeanour of gravity suitable to the occasion, and who said :

'It is a question of hours now, I am sorry to tell you. The doctor is here and has kindly promised to stay until the end ; but there is nothing more to be done. Of course we were more or less prepared for this ; still it has come more suddenly than we expected.'

Ida went into the dying man's room, where
Lady Elizabeth was seated, weeping help-
lessly. Two old servants were also present and
were also crying. These had some right and
reason to be sorrowful ; for authority was
passing into fresh hands ; and who can tell
how a new master may think fit to deal with
his dependents ? But the doctor, who stood
by the bedside, listening to the slow,
laborious breathing of the old man, glanced
furtively at his watch from time to time,
and probably hoped that he might not be
detained much longer. His unspoken wish
was doubtless echoed by Wilfrid, and also
in some degree by Ida, who could only hold
Lady Elizabeth's hand and regret her in-
capacity to say anything worth saying.
One of the greatest inconveniences connected
with the body to which we are bound is
the extreme difficulty which we generally
experience in getting rid of it.

Poor old Mr. Chaine, having a strong
constitution, could neither obtain his own
release, nor release those who were waiting

for it, until after sunset. But at length the doctor bent over him for a moment, stepped back and whispered a few words to one of the servants; whereupon Ida rose and withdrew noiselessly, followed by her brother-in-law.

She was naturally a good deal moved; so that Wilfrid's first words jarred upon her nerves and shocked her.

'You must be famishing,' he said. 'Won't you come down to the dining-room and have something to eat before you go?'

'I am not at all hungry, thank you,' she answered, 'and I would rather stay, if I can be of any use.'

'Oh, I don't think you could do much good by staying; my mother will be all right as soon as she has had a comfortable cry. I will let you know if she wishes to see you; but I dare say the best plan will be to leave her to herself until after the funeral. Are you sure you won't have a glass of wine and a biscuit?'

He looked almost jubilant. As a matter

of fact, he felt so; and it was either a failing or a virtue of his that he was not clever at dissimulation in cases where his own immediate interests did not seem to require that he should dissemble. Yet, if he had only known it, it might possibly have been to his interest to conciliate his sister-in-law, who turned away from him in silent disgust and bent her steps homewards, wondering by what strange fatality it had come to pass that Mr. Chaine — a chivalrous, scrupulous gentleman in his narrow way — had been afflicted with sons who displayed neither chivalry nor scruples nor even that common decency of behaviour which is the outward sign of a gentleman.

CHAPTER XXV

THE NEW BROOM

OLD Mr. Chaine's body was deposited beside those of his forefathers in the family vault with all the pomp and circumstance which belonged to his station. It is usual in these days to express a wish that one's funeral obsequies may be conducted as unexpensively and unostentatiously as possible, and it is also usual, on the part of the survivors, to disregard that wish; so that, upon the whole, perhaps the best plan is to say nothing about it. Mr. Chaine, at all events, had said nothing about it, and consequently the inheritor of his estates, though a man of frugal mind, recognised the necessity of doing things upon a handsome and liberal scale. Relations, near and far, were duly summoned to attend the ceremony; the tenantry were given to understand that their presence would be expected; and the St. Albyn's undertaker received instructions to make every preparation that might, in his judgment, be deemed adequate to the occasion.

'After all,' thought Wilfrid to himself, 'this kind of thing must be regarded as a sort of social legacy - duty. It's infernal nonsense, and one doesn't exactly enjoy being robbed all round; still it would be a mistake to start by acquiring a character for stinginess, and the legacy is there—a solid consolation for the sorrowful and the bereaved.'

The legacy, no doubt, was there—he saw it all around him when he took his place, as chief mourner, in the imposing procession which wound its slow way from Chaine Court towards the gray, weather-beaten tower of the parish church, whence the tolling of a cracked bell gave notice to the outer world that one more Chaine had gone to his eternal home—but what he was thinking of uneasily as he paced, with bowed head, behind the

coffin, was that the disposition which the
dead man had made of his personal property
was as yet a matter of absolute uncertainty.
With the payment of a large jointure he
must, of course, expect to be saddled; but
what about Mrs. John and her equitable,
if not legal, claims? Wilfrid did most
sincerely hope that his father had not been
guilty of that kind of generosity which
hardly merits the name of generosity, since
it can only be carried into effect at the
expense of other people.

He looked grave and melancholy and
altogether respectable when he knelt in the
little church and when he stood, afterwards,
at the entrance of the vault where Lady
Elizabeth and Ida, in their deep mourning
robes, had stationed themselves; but a rite
which saddens and softens most of us did
not appeal to him, for the simple reason
that he was not listening to it. He scarcely
believed in the immortality of the soul; he
did not believe at all in the resurrection of
the body; his feeling was that the deceased

had had his fair share of the good things of this world; he was eager to have done with conventional tributes to the past, to give his attention to the present and to find out what sort of a prospect there was for the future.

As soon as the ceremony was at an end he touched Ida on the elbow and whispered: 'You will come back to the house with my mother, I suppose, won't you? You may as well be present at the reading of the will.'

'I will come if Lady Elizabeth wants me,' answered Ida, drawing back a step, for the whole scene had produced an impression upon her which it had failed to produce upon him, and she was repelled by the heartlessness of his manner even more than by his words. 'I don't think there can be any necessity for me to hear the will read, though.'

'There is no question of necessity; but I should think it might probably interest you. However, pray do just as you feel inclined.'

Ida's personal inclinations would have prompted her to go straight home. She knew that she had been sufficiently provided for and was not curious, at the moment, to learn what provision had been made for others. Still it was impossible to refuse the request of Lady Elizabeth, who presently took her by the arm and led her out to the carriage which had brought them both to the church, saying :

'My dear, I want you to see me through the next hour, if you will. Neither you nor I know yet what income we have to count upon, and Wilfrid thinks we ought to hear all about it. Most likely he is right, and I dare say it won't take very long.'

As a matter of fact, it did take rather a long time, for Mr. Chaine's will filled as many folio pages as a careful and conscientious family lawyer had been able to devote to it. The framer of this monumental specimen of legal literature read his work aloud in the library to a tolerably large circle of listeners, most of whom had only a very vague idea of

what he was talking about. The one thing
that seemed evident was that the deceased
gentleman must have lived well within his
income; for there was an interminable list of
charities to which he bequeathed sums varying
from fifty to five hundred pounds. Ida soon
ceased to lend an attentive ear to the lawyer's
monotonous droning; but Lady Elizabeth,
who had been weeping disconsolately since
daybreak, and who was in truth as disconsolate
as her nature would permit her to be, retained
sufficient possession of her faculties to follow
him more or less accurately, and heaved
a sigh of relief when it became clear to her
that, so far as she was concerned, her dear
husband had done the right thing. Whether
he had done the right thing as regarded
his daughter-in-law was, however, a question
which admitted of two opinions. The White
House until death or re-marriage and forty
thousand pounds down! — it certainly did
sound a trifle extravagant. And if that was
Lady Elizabeth's view, it was still more the
view of her son, whose jaw dropped and who

had much ado to swallow down the bad words
which found their way to the tip of his tongue.
Forty thousand pounds, in addition to all
that money so senselessly squandered upon
charities !—oh, hang it all !

Wilfrid did not confine himself to inwardly
hanging it all, he used much more forcible
unuttered language.   Nevertheless, he preserved a calm, albeit chastened exterior, and
it was the subject of general remark that he
behaved uncommonly well under circumstances
which, as everybody felt, must be somewhat
trying for him.   When the relations had taken
their leave and had been despatched to the
railway station, he approached his mother and
Ida, saying, with a smile :

'I don't know whether you understood the
meaning of all that legal gibberish.'

'Oh yes,' answered Lady Elizabeth, 'I
think so.   It was much what your dear father
always led me to expect, and he seems to have
been guided entirely by custom and precedent.'

Wilfrid glanced at Ida, who remained silent,
before he rejoined, 'Well, I don't know about

precedent; the circumstances, you see, are unprecedented. The White House, I believe, has always hitherto been considered as a dower-house, and I don't recollect any previous instance of so large a sum as forty thousand pounds being left to any member of the family. Still I have no doubt that my father meant to act justly, and I hope that, when we have looked into his affairs, we shall find ourselves with a sufficient sum in hand to pay all bequests.'

'You may be quite sure of that,' returned Lady Elizabeth, with a touch of resentment. 'Your father would never have thought of disposing of money which was not in his possession to dispose of. As for me, I knew all along that I should not inherit the White House. If John had lived, it would have been assigned to you, I believe.'

Wilfrid nodded and presently changed the subject, merely remarking: 'I am glad that you are both satisfied; I wasn't sure that you would be.'

Ida, for her part, was not quite sure that she was satisfied, now that her attention

had been drawn in that marked manner to
the exceptional liberality with which she
had been treated. Was it, after all, fair
that she should take so much from a family
to which she was allied by no tie of con-
sanguinity? She saw plainly enough that
Wilfrid did not think it fair, and before she
went away she found an opportunity of telling him that she had no wish to despoil
anybody.

'I am afraid,' said she, while he was con-
ducting her through the hall, 'that Mr.
Chaine's will makes me more of a burden
upon you and Lady Elizabeth than I ought to
be. If that is so, you must understand that I
would much rather resign a part of what he
has given me. I know nothing about these
matters; but I know that I can live upon a
very small income and that it would be no
pleasure to me to be made rich at your expense.
I suppose a will must be obeyed; only there
is nothing to prevent me from handing the
greater part of what I shall receive back to
you or your mother, is there?'

'Nothing in the world,' answered Wilfrid, smiling, 'except the force of public opinion—which may be regarded as invincible. You are very kind; but we can no more accept money from you than we could have allowed you to starve, if your name hadn't appeared in the will. And really I have no idea what the amount of my father's personal property is; it is possible that forty thousand pounds may not make so large a hole in it as I should have imagined. To speak frankly, I think he went a little beyond what is usual in leaving the White House to you; but, under the conditions he has named, that must revert to us eventually, and may, for anything that I know to the contrary, revert to us very soon.'

There was a certain veiled suggestion of impertinence in the last words which made the blood rise to Ida's cheeks and caused her to bid her brother-in-law farewell somewhat curtly. Yet what he had said was not without effect upon her subsequent meditations, nor could she help perceiving that, if at any time she should feel disposed to marry again, she would not only injure nobody by so doing, but would confer a positive benefit upon at least one individual. And why should she not marry a second time? Mr. Chaine had foreseen and approved of the contingency; assuredly she owed no vow of perpetual widowhood to John's memory; the sole obstacle was the rather important one that the only man whom she could ever think of marrying had no intention of asking her to be his wife. She was persuaded that he had no such intention, and she was angry with herself for having speculated, even in that vague fashion, upon an event which could never come to pass. 'There is no help for it,' she murmured disconsolately as she went to bed that night; 'of course they couldn't accept money from me, and of course I shall have to inhabit this house till the end of my days. It will be just like me to live to a hundred and keep two generations out of their own!'

But she was to some extent reassured on the following day by a visit from Lady Elizabeth, whose spirits had revived and who candidly

avowed that nothing would have induced her
to dwell in a dower-house, had such a residence
been placed at her disposal.

'Between ourselves, my dear,' the old lady
said, 'I have always rather hated the country.
What I mean to do now is to look out for a
small house in Mayfair, where my friends can
come and see me and where I shall be what
the French call *dans le mouvement.* "This
world is all a fleeting show," as the hymn so
truly says; still there is no crime that I know
of in looking on at the show, and I feel that
I am fitted by nature to play the part of a
benevolent spectator. If my rent isn't too
high, I daresay I shall manage to toddle off to
Cannes or some such place for the winter, and
I shall continue to subscribe to the Church
Missionary Society and the other admirable
undertakings which I have made a point of
supporting for so many years. I don't profess
to be a saint; but I am a harmless sort of
sinner, when all's said and done.'

It was evident that Lady Elizabeth had
already overcome her grief sufficiently to take

an almost childish delight in her liberty, and
it was also, happily, evident that she entertained no sort of grudge against her daughter-
in-law. She was not precisely devoted to Ida,
who was rather too cold and reserved to suit
her taste; but it was a matter of absolute
necessity for her to impart her wishes and plans
to somebody, and if Ida had no other merit
she was at least a fairly good listener.

Thus it came to pass that Mrs. John Chaine's
presence was requested and required every
afternoon at the Court, and that she was made
the recipient of certain confidences which
angered, without surprising, her. Not that
Lady Elizabeth had any complaint to make of
Wilfrid—she said he was most considerate and
anxious to be of assistance to her in the
management of her affairs—only it transpired
that he had no notion of offering her a home,
and that he had even asked her to fix some
date on which it would be convenient to her to
remove her personal belongings.

'I think he wants to put the house in order
and get some painting and papering done,' the

old lady explained, with pathetic eagerness to exculpate the new owner. 'It is quite right and natural that he should, and he can't set to work so long as I am here and so long as the servants will persist in coming to me for orders.'

Nevertheless she could not quite conceal the fact that she felt a little hurt. 'I would take myself off to-morrow,' she declared, 'if I didn't think that I am really of some use to him by staying on for a time. After all, a bachelor doesn't know how to keep house, and one can hardly trust a housekeeper to make him comfortable.'

'Of course not,' agreed Ida. 'I must say I should have thought that while he remained unmarried——'

'Oh, he won't remain unmarried long,' interrupted Lady Elizabeth; 'he couldn't if he would, you know—it's out of the question in his position. At one time I was in hopes that he was taking a fancy to my young friend Violet Stanton, who, by the way, came to see me yesterday; but he doesn't seem to have troubled himself much about her in London, and, as far as I can make out, my niece Anne Hartlepool, with whom she has been staying, has been trying to arrange another match for her. However, it is quite upon the cards that Wilfrid may make amends for past neglect now. I shall be glad if he does, because Violet is a nice sort of girl, besides being pretty. Don't you think so?'

Ida certainly thought Miss Stanton pretty, but was hardly well enough acquainted with her to say whether she was nice or not. At the same time, it appeared to her probable that the girl was far too nice to become the wife of Wilfrid Chaine; and she was confirmed in this opinion a few days later when she found her drinking tea with Lady Elizabeth, and when, after half an hour or so of general conversation, the young lady obligingly offered to drive her home.

Violet, on her side, had always entertained a strong feeling of interest and curiosity, not unmixed with admiration, for Ida Chaine; so that the two women were no sooner seated,

side by side, in the pony-cart than the younger
began to make remarks of a leading character.
There is never any difficulty about introducing
a subject that you wish to discuss, because it
really does not matter in the least whether
you introduce it cleverly or clumsily, and
Violet soon elicited from her companion an
emphatic and somewhat unexpected condemnation of *mariages de convenance*. Considering that Mrs. John Chaine had undoubtedly
made such a marriage, and that it had resulted,
upon the whole, in the promotion of her
worldly interests, it seemed rather strange that
she should express herself so forcibly; but
Ida, who was thinking rather of her questioner's
case than of her own, was determined not to
neglect an opportunity of speaking a word in
season.

‘ I am quite certain,’ said she, ‘ that a woman
who puts herself up for sale in the marriage
market parts with her happiness as well as her
self-respect. Luxuries are pleasant things—it
isn’t worth while to deny that; only, like all
other pleasant things, they have their price,

and the perpetual society of a man whom you don't love, yet must pretend to love, is too long a price to pay for all the houses and horses and dresses in England.'

'I don't see why there should be any need for pretence,' objected Violet. 'I can understand that if one had ever been in love with anybody one might feel bound to pretend and believe, if one could, that one hadn't changed ; but there's no reason why one shouldn't start with a mutual agreement to put love out of the question.'

'Except that no man would care to marry upon those terms. There is sure to be love on one side, and sooner or later there is sure to be hate on both sides, unless it is either returned or simulated. I thought as you do once ; but I know better now.'

This speech was followed by the pause which inevitably succeeds half confessions. Violet could only hold her peace, and Ida was not inclined to be more explicit. When the latter spoke again it was only to remark upon the want of kindly feeling which Wilfrid had displayed towards his mother, and to express her personal dislike for the man, whom she stigmatised as selfish and calculating.

Violet did not take up the cudgels on his behalf. 'Oh, I daresay he is much the same as other people,' she said indifferently; 'we are all selfish, and we should simply be trodden under foot by our neighbours if we weren't. Only of course some of us are hypocrites and some are honest.'

'I doubt whether Wilfrid is among the honest ones,' observed Ida, not caring to combat so rough and ready a classification of the human race.

But she could not get the girl to betray any interest at all in the question of Wilfrid's honesty, nor was she able, during the short time that their drive lasted, to discover what likelihood there was of Lady Elizabeth's hopes being fulfilled. What she did discover was that, for some reason or other, Violet Stanton was disposed to be influenced by her; and she was glad of that, both because she was badly off for friends and because she felt it

to be nothing short of a sacred duty to preserve any fellow-creature whom it might be in
her power to preserve from falling into such a
fatal error as she herself had committed. Her
parting words, therefore, took the form of an
invitation which was accepted with alacrity.

'I should like awfully to come and see you
sometimes, if I may,' Violet declared. 'I
have been wanting for ever so long to know
you better; only I didn't think you would
particularly care to know me.'

Thus was laid the foundation of a friendship which proved more lasting than the
friendships of women are commonly supposed
to be.

CHAPTER XXVI

A CHANGE OF REGIMENTS

VIOLET STANTON, like a great many other people who behave with a certain show of audacity and independence, was constitutionally shy. In making friends with Mrs. John Chaine she had no intention of unbosoming herself or of seeking advice, and although the two ladies speedily became intimate, neither of them inquired or learnt much about the other during the ripening of their intimacy. As for Sir Harvey Amherst, his name was not so much as mentioned between them. Violet, of course, was thinking about him pretty constantly, wondering how soon he would put in an appearance and what she should say to him when he did; but her allusions to a subject which possessed considerable interest for her were so vague that Ida naturally misinter-

preted them. The latter, perceiving what
indeed was evident enough, that her young
friend contemplated an alliance recommended
solely by sordid incentives, took it for granted
that Wilfrid Chaine was the potential husband
in question and wasted a good deal of time
and eloquence in depreciating that comparatively harmless personage. It was chiefly
about him that she discoursed while Violet sat
beside her tea-table or accompanied her on her
visits to the cottages of the poor, and she was
not a little puzzled by the unaffected indif-
ference with which her accusations against
him were received.

She was also constrained to feel some doubt
as to the seriousness of Wilfrid's intentions.
He dropped in one afternoon when Violet
happened to be with her, and although he was
certainly attentive to Miss Stanton and looked
at her in a way which to feminine eyes was
unquestionably significant, it did not seem
certain that his sentiments had reached a more
decisive stage than that of mere admiration.
He was, in fact, far more preoccupied with his

personal projects and arrangements than a lover has any business to be. He was going away for a time, he said, in order that the house might be thoroughly cleaned up and necessary repairs effected; he hoped that, during his absence, Ida would do him the favour to send for any cut flowers that she might want from the conservatories, and he graciously extended the same invitation to Miss Stanton.

'Your mother is leaving you, then, I suppose?' said Ida.

'Yes; she is going to stay with some of her people for a time, and after that I believe she intends going abroad for the winter. There's a lot of furniture belonging to her which will have to be removed, and until that is out of the way I shan't be able to get things straight; but I daresay I shall have managed to settle myself down more or less comfortably by the time that the hunting season begins. I hope to have the mingled pleasure and humiliation of being cut down by you before Christmas, Miss Stanton.'

'It won't be my fault if you are denied that treat,' returned Violet; 'and it isn't my fault that I only possess one horse, while you, I suppose, will have half a dozen.'

She remarked subsequently to her hostess that no hunting man would have made such a silly speech, and that she would believe more in Mr. Wilfrid Chaine's sporting capabilities when she should have seen him go; but she did not concur in Ida's denunciation of him for 'turning his mother out of doors.'

'I am very sorry that Lady Elizabeth is going,' she said; 'she is a dear old thing, and I shall miss her. But I think she is quite right to lose no time in leaving a house which doesn't belong to her any more. I should do just the same in her place.'

Upon the whole, she appeared to survey Wilfrid and his proceedings from an altogether detached point of view—which was the less surprising inasmuch as that was in truth her mental attitude with regard to him. She neither liked nor disliked the man whom Ida attacked so persistently; she was seldom brought into contact with him, and his departure made no sort of difference in her life. The departure of Lady Elizabeth, which took place simultaneously with his, did make a difference, and when the time came to bid farewell to the kind-hearted old woman who had been so good a friend to her she shed a few irrepressible tears ; but it will be readily understood that all her emotions were temporarily blunted by the thought of the crisis in her own life which she knew to be at hand, and that she had much the same difficulty in forgetting Sir Harvey Amherst as we all have in forgetting an obstinate fit of toothache. The only cure for that troublesome ailment which can be confidently recommended is to have the aching tooth extracted ; but many people shrink from a remedy which they imagine to be almost as bad as the complaint, and it may be that not a few young ladies, situated as Violet was, would have hesitated, as she did, to relieve themselves of all further anxiety by the simple method of deciding to reject Sir Harvey. She, at all events, felt

quite unable to come to an immediate decision, one way or the other; nor was she disturbed by any news of her suitor, who in fact
was still amusing himself quite contentedly
in fashionable circles.

The clerical society of St. Albyn's always
affected to ignore the movements of the garrison, and was wont to assume an air of
languid surprise on being informed that this
regiment had arrived or that that had left the
city. Nevertheless, as Mrs. Stanton would
often say apologetically, 'one really can't help
hearing things,' and so both she and her
daughter were duly apprised of the advent of
the 90th Hussars to replace the 22d, ordered
abroad. To Mrs. Stanton this was not an
event of much importance; but it afforded a
little pleasurable excitement to Violet, who
remembered that she had the honour of being
acquainted with a certain young lieutenant
in that distinguished corps, and that he had
treated her somewhat cavalierly on the occasion of their last meeting. She was willing to
pardon that rudeness of his (feeling that it

had not been wholly without excuse), and she determined to give him a kind and friendly welcome as soon as he should show his sense of what was due to her by calling to ask for it.

But it seemed that the young man was either ignorant or deliberately neglectful of social obligations, for he abstained from paying his respects, although Violet soon found out that he had been at the White House and had even taken the liberty of talking about her there.

'Hubert was here yesterday,' Ida told her, with a slightly amused look. 'What did you do to him in London to make him so angry with you?'

'I am sorry if I have offended him,' answered Violet loftily; 'but my conscience doesn't accuse me of having done anything worse than failing to notice his presence when he came to tea with Lady Hartlepool one afternoon. No doubt that was a dire affront; still I daresay it won't have done him much harm to be taught that he isn't quite the only person in the world.'

'Oh, he is aware—not to say painfully aware — of the existence of other persons,' returned Ida, laughing. 'He is aware, for instance, of the existence of a certain Sir Harvey Amherst, whom I am ashamed to say that I had never heard of until Hubert told me about him. I suppose I ought to have heard of him too, since he represents a division of the county in Parliament.'

'Sir Harvey Amherst,' said Violet, without changing colour, 'is not only a member of Parliament, but a reasonable, sensible being. I know him quite as well as I know Mr. Hubert Chaine; but I am sure that it would never occur to him to think himself slighted if I happened to be talking to somebody else when he entered a room.'

Ida laughed again and changed the subject. She saw now—it is not impossible that she may have been intended to see—how the land lay, and it was doubtless due to her initiative that Mrs. and Miss Stanton were invited, two days later, to dine quite quietly with the Dean of St. Albyn's. The Dean explained in his note that he only expected his daughter and one or two others. Owing to the recent loss which they had sustained, neither he nor she could entertain friends at present; but he hoped that, if Mrs. Stanton had nothing better to do, she would kindly consent to join a very small family gathering.

The gathering consisted of the Dean and Ida, Canon and Mrs. Pickersgill, Hubert Chaine and an elderly bachelor parson who held a living in the neighbourhood. Its composition did not appear to hold out much promise of hilarity; but it probably served the purpose of its designer, inasmuch as it rendered a temporary partnership between Hubert and Violet inevitable.

The chins of the young man and the young woman were alike raised to a high level as they moved, arm in arm, towards the dining-room, and during the first ten minutes or so their intercourse was of an elaborately polite and formal character; but at length Violet, who was not half as angry as he was, found this dignified demeanour too irksome to be

kept up, and asked him point-blank what was
the matter with him.

'You needn't tell me that nothing is the
matter,' she added, 'because I can't believe
that you would take such pains to be disagreeable about nothing.'

'Am I disagreeable?' returned Hubert,
raising his eyebrows. 'I thought I was only
rather dull.'

'It is the easiest thing in the world to be
both. Now will you kindly tell me how I
have incurred your displeasure?'

Of course he protested that she had done
nothing of the sort, and of course he eventually gave her to understand, by means of
roundabout statements, that her behaviour in
London had shocked and grieved him. Owing
to the restrictions imposed by custom upon
the exercise of free speech, it naturally took
him rather a long time to make his meaning
clear and to receive in return what he rightly
took to be an assurance that his neighbour
was not yet affianced to Sir Harvey Amherst;
but between soup and dessert that degree of

mutual comprehension was arrived at, and a vast improvement had taken place in Hubert's temper and spirits when Violet closed a discussion of a nature which she had more than once before held with him by remarking:

'Well, you and I are not of one mind about these matters, and when people are not of one mind it is only a waste of time and patience to argue. Let us try to find some subject upon which we do agree. Do you mean to come out cubbing with us this autumn?'

'Rather!' answered Hubert, with a brightened countenance; 'I'd sooner lose a month in the middle of the season than miss the cubhunting—especially if you come out. Don't you mind getting up in the dark?'

'If I did, I should get precious little hunting at any time of the year. Besides, I should do it for the sake of my horse even if I didn't do it for my own. I am convinced that nothing is so good for a horse as getting him into good, hard condition by the beginning of the season. If you don't go to work with him by degrees the chances

are that you will have him on the sick-list
at the very time when you need him most.'

Hubert had sundry countervailing considerations to put forward, and both he and
his interlocutor became so engrossed in a
topic which might possibly not be found
engrossing by the general reader, that they
eagerly resumed it the moment that they met
again in the drawing-room after dinner. For
the time being they almost forgot that they
belonged to opposite sexes, and quite forgot
that, a few hours earlier, they had had no intention of ever making friends again.

Other people, meanwhile, were fully alive
to phenomena which, as all experience shows,
only admit of one interpretation. Mrs.
Pickersgill had her eye upon them, and Mrs.
Pickersgill would have had something to say
about them both but for the unlucky circumstance that she was seated beside Violet's
mother. As the good lady could hardly point
out to Mrs. Stanton what a very vulgar style
of flirtation her daughter had seen fit to
adopt, she was fain to console herself by

lamenting the indiscreet and almost indecent behaviour of her hostess.

'Of course you have heard about her and young Mayne,' she said.

Mrs. Stanton had heard nothing, but intimated that she would not object to receiving any information that might be vouchsafed to her.

'Oh, there's no concealment about it,' the other old lady returned; 'I must say for Mrs. Chaine that she has a fine contempt for public opinion. The young man is at her house almost every day, and really one feels that, for the sake of her own reputation, the sooner she announces her engagement the better. We all know what her motives were for marrying that unfortunate husband of hers, and we all know that she threw over Arthur Mayne in the first instance; so that her cynicism can't be called altogether surprising. Still I do think it would have shown better feeling to wait just a little longer. There is something so shockingly callous in marrying at the earliest opportu-

nity upon the dead man's money—especially
when you remember what the circumstances
were which drove him, as one may say, to his
death!'

'But he was killed by an accident, wasn't
he?' asked Mrs. Stanton.

'So they say; the details have been kept
rather suspiciously quiet. But whether he
died by his own hand or not, there is no
getting over the facts that his widow has been
left very well off, and that he would have
been alive now if her conduct had not goaded
him into committing an act of insanity. As
for poor young Mayne, one can only pity him
and hope that he may be more fortunate than
his predecessor.'

Mrs. Stanton was not more ill-natured than
other old women and not half as ill-natured
as some; but she was immensely interested,
as they all are, without exception, in other
people's business, and this frequently caused
her to neglect her own. Consequently she
spent a pleasant evening, and was troubled by
no anxiety with regard to her daughter, whom

Mrs. Pickersgill, on the other hand, perceived to be in a fair way towards getting into serious trouble. But Mrs. Pickersgill, to be sure, had always foreseen that a girl who had been allowed, as Violet Stanton had been, to run wild would get into serious trouble sooner or later.

'It will come to this,' she told her husband, after they had taken their leave, 'that I shall be obliged to strike the Stantons' name off our invitation-list. I try to make every allowance that I can; but it doesn't do for us to forget that we live in a garrison town, and certainly it would never do for us to permit garrison manners to be exhibited in our garden.'

Ignorant of the awful doom with which she was threatened, Violet went home in very good spirits and remarked casually to her mother: 'You will have to come and look on at a polo-match to-morrow. You won't enjoy watching the game; but you will enjoy meeting your friends, because everybody is to be there, and I promised Mr. Chaine that we would be among the spectators.'

'Are you quite sure that everybody is
going, my dear?' inquired Mrs. Stanton; for
she was in a constant state of nervous alarm
lest she should be caught doing something
that everybody else didn't do.

'Well, the Dean is going,' answered Violet,
'and so is Mrs. Chaine. If that isn't enough
to give an air of respectability to the proceedings, I don't know what is.'

After what she had heard that evening,
Mrs. Stanton was not quite so sure as to
the value of Ida's patronage, and she observed
that it was rather soon for any member of the
Chaine family to appear at public entertain-
ments; still the Dean was, of course, a tower
of strength. Moreover, she had been informed
of the candidature of Sir Harvey Amherst;
so that she was free from any dread of so
hopeless a detrimental as Hubert.

The result of this somewhat exaggerated
sense of security on Mrs. Stanton's part was
that she duly escorted her daughter, on the
following afternoon, to the field adjoining
the barracks, and very glad she was to see

that the Army was, for once, in full enjoyment of the benevolent patronage of the
Church. The apron and gaiters of the Dean
were flanked by those of Bishop Jenkinson;
the Honourable Mrs. Jenkinson was seated
in state beneath an awning, with Ida Chaine
on her right hand and Mrs. Pickersgill on
her left; the county families had sent repre-
sentatives; in short, everything tended to
show that the meeting was a select and
aristocratic one. And when Mrs. Stanton
had been introduced to the Colonel of the
regiment, who found a chair for her close
behind Mrs. Jenkinson's, she felt quite glad
that she had come.

'This is much better than one of those
horrid cricket-matches, where one is expected
to like rubbing shoulders with the butcher
and the baker and the candlestick-maker,' she
whispered to Violet, who returned placidly:

'I told you you would enjoy yourself.'

Violet also proposed and expected to enjoy
herself. She knew very little about polo;
but she knew almost as much as she thought

she knew about horsemanship, and it was a
satisfaction to her to notice with what skill
and judgment Hubert rode his clever little
pony. A place was assigned to her beside
Ida, whose attention she drew to certain
niceties of handling which might otherwise
have failed to be apparent to the uninformed
mind, and who, for half an hour, derived a
good deal of quiet amusement from noting
the circumstance that all Miss Stanton's
criticisms on the game bore reference to one
player.

Now, nobody will think of denying that
accidents may occur to the best of riders,
and that the wisest of ponies, if wheeled
round abruptly, is liable to slip up and come
down; consequently there was nothing surprising or discreditable in the fact that, after
a time, both Hubert and his mount had a
rather nasty tumble. Ida half rose from
her seat, drawing in her breath; but Violet
said calmly, 'Oh, that's nothing,' and remained
unmoved until she saw that, although the
pony had scrambled on to his legs again,

Hubert still lay where he had fallen. Then
she turned pale and, gripping her neighbour's
arm with unconscious violence, asked in an
awe - struck whisper, 'Has he broken his
neck?'

There was not much use in putting such
a question to Ida; but, regardless of what the
assembled company might think of her, she
ran down, a minute or two later, to put it
to the regimental surgeon, who happened to
be upon the spot and who was assisting to
remove the injured man. By this precipitate
action she obtained a reply which was at once
reassuring and humiliating.

'Lord bless your soul, no!' answered the
military practitioner, whose manners were not
quite as refined as they might have been;
'he's only knocked out of time. He has
dislocated his shoulder, and I'm not sure that
he hasn't broken his collar-bone; but there's
nothing to make such a fuss about. Please
tell the ladies that it's all right—and perhaps
you wouldn't mind standing on one side. We
shall get him into barracks rather more quickly

if we don't have to force our way through a gaping crowd.'

If anything could have added to Violet's vexation with herself it would have been her knowledge that this brief colloquy had been distinctly heard by the interesting youth on the hurdle, who looked up at her and smiled, murmuring something which she did not catch. She returned to the tent with pink cheeks, conscious of the disapproving stare of Mrs. Pickersgill and the other ladies, and as soon as she had regained her place she was careful to explain to Ida in an audible voice that, having witnessed a good many spills in the hunting-field, she had thought she might be of use, in case anything serious had been the matter.

But this explanation was not accepted. It was received with a chilling silence which was only broken by Mrs. Stanton's subdued and annoyed protest of, ' Violet, dear, I *wish* you wouldn't do such extraordinary things ! '

And what was even more trying was that, when the game had been resumed and public

attention had been diverted from her, Ida
squeezed her hand, laughing and saying:
'Never mind! there's nothing to be ashamed
of in a humane impulse, and he shall be well
nursed, I promise you.'

'I don't care whether he is well or badly
nursed,' returned Violet ungratefully; 'it
wouldn't have made any difference to me
if he had been killed.   What business has
a man who has only put his shoulder out
to sham dead in that way!'

Whereat her friend was cruel enough to
laugh more than ever.

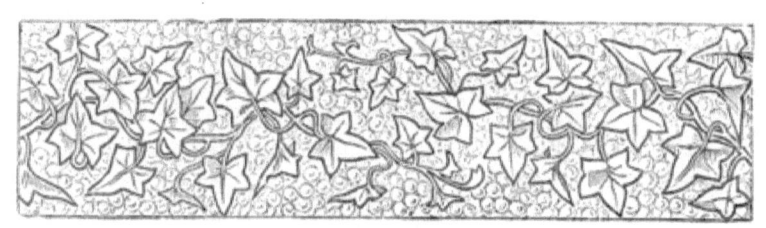

CHAPTER XXVII

THE INCONSEQUENCE OF MRS. CHAINE

THE doctor's surmise was verified with regard
to Hubert Chaine, who, on subsequent and
closer examination, was found to have both
dislocated his shoulder and broken his collar-
bone; but of course neither of these injuries
was of an alarming character, nor was there
any real necessity for all the care that his
sister-in-law was pleased to take of him during
the few days of his enforced detention in bed.
Still it was very kind of her to drive in every
morning and spend so many hours in amusing
him by reading the newspapers and talking,
and he was duly grateful to her for her
sympathy. Perhaps he was all the more
grateful to her because he did not obtain
the full measure of that boon to which he
was fairly entitled from other quarters. The

Dean, it is true, sent to inquire, as did Canon
Pickersgill and others who had witnessed the
mishap; but Miss Stanton saw fit to neglect
what may surely be looked upon as a customary and formal piece of attention, and this
struck him as being rather unkind.   He asked
Ida whether it wasn't rather unkind, and she
replied that she quite thought so.

'All the same,' she added, 'you must
remember that Violet showed her anxiety
about you at the time in a very conspicuous
way.   You might allow her credit for that,
and also for being a little bit disconcerted
at having made an exhibition of herself upon
insufficient grounds.'

The poor invalid rose to the fly with the
alacrity which our innocent sex never fails
to display under such circumstances.   Had
she really made any exhibition of herself?
Did Ida think that she was conscious of having
made an exhibition of herself?   Was it possible that she cared a brass farthing whether
he had fractured his vertebral column or only
an insignificant clavicle?   Ida deemed this

to be well within the limits of possibility,
and said as much. In short, she very soon
turned the unfortunate young man morally
inside out, and heard all about Sir Harvey
Amherst's and Wilfrid's pretensions, as well
as those of a humbler and less sanguine
individual. And in truth it was no bad
thing for him to have secured an ally at
the price of having gratified that feminine
curiosity which it is always the wisest plan
to gratify, if possible. He obtained the usual
reward, and was confidently assured that his
case was far from being hopeless.

'You must have patience' was the advice
of his sage counsellor. 'Very likely she
might refuse you now, because, you see,
there is no denying that you are hardly in
a position to marry upon your present income.
But if she cares for you — as I believe she
does — she certainly won't marry that old
man or Wilfrid either, and when once they
have proposed and been rejected you may come
forward with more safety. Why shouldn't she
wait until you are a little better off? It is

only what hundreds and thousands of girls have to do; and I am sure you will no more mind denying yourself a few luxuries, when the time comes, than she will.'

Hubert, it need scarcely be said, declared his entire willingness to subsist upon bread and water with the object of his affections. Had he supposed himself incapable of that trifling sacrifice, he would have been almost as abnormal a young man as if he had in reality been capable of it. And his prospective self-abnegation won him the unrestricted admiration and esteem of a lady whose influence over him seemed to be due rather to precept than to example.

'Leave it to me, and don't be downhearted,' said she. 'I know very well that Violet is dying to hear how you are getting on; I know very well that in a few days' time she won't be able to stand it any longer, and will have to come over and see me. Then I shall fight your battle for you as well as I can. Only I warn you that she won't strike her colours at the first shot; you

mustn't expect that. What you will do, if
you have any common sense, will be to avoid
her for a time, and let her imagine that you
are resigned to your hard fate.'

Well, it was easy for a bedridden man to
act upon that advice, and Ida's astute prog-
nostication was fulfilled when Miss Stanton
rode across the fields to the White House,
one afternoon, to look up her friend about
tea-time.

Not, indeed, that she had any questions
to ask as to the condition of the disabled
warrior, for it soon transpired that she knew
all about that and was quite free from
uneasiness on his account; but she was
anxious — or at least she said she was — to
find out whether she had offended her friend
in any way. 'Because,' said she, 'I hear that
you have been in St. Albyn's every day for the
last week, and you have never come near us.'

'I haven't had the time,' answered Ida.
'I have been nursing poor Hubert, as I
promised you that I would, and I always try
to keep my promises. No; you haven't

offended me yet, though I daresay you will
before long. That is, if you do what, from
all that you have told me, I am afraid you
are bent upon doing.'

Violet, who had pugnacious instincts,
opened her eyes very wide, and looked
quite ready to accept the challenge. 'I
don't know what you mean,' she declared;
'I am not bent upon doing anything disgraceful that I am aware of.'

'Ah, that depends upon what may be
considered disgraceful. Sir Harvey Amherst
won't do anything disgraceful if he marries
you—he will only make a fool of himself;
but can you, or any responsible being,
seriously believe that there is nothing to be
ashamed of in marrying an old man for no
other reason than that he is a rich old man?'

'I can guess who told you about Sir
Harvey Amherst,' remarked Violet, with an
angry tremor in her voice. 'Probably he
told you no more than the truth; still I
really don't see what business it is of his,
or—or——'

'Or of mine either? Well, he doesn't pretend that it is any business of his. He is not putting himself forward as the old gentleman's rival, and I dare say that, if I hadn't cross-examined him, he would never have mentioned a rumour which I suppose it is permitted to him to regard as a rather melancholy one. As for me, I am fond enough of you to brave the risk of being thought impertinent and interfering, and if any words of mine can restrain you from making the most miserable mistake that a woman can make, they shall be spoken.'

Now, that kind of speech does not come over and above well from a woman who has notoriously married for money and who has been left a widow with ample means.

'It is all very well for you to take up the sentimental side of the question,' Violet felt constrained to remark; 'you are safe in harbour, and you can sit at your ease and advise other people not to put out to sea. Still I should have thought——'

She had not quite the courage or the cruelty to finish her sentence; but Ida calmly finished it for her.

'You would have thought that, considering what I myself did, I should have had rather more sympathy with you. Well, it is just on that account that I do sympathise with you and that I want to save you. When I married John Chaine I hadn't the slightest idea of what it was that I was consenting to, and I don't believe that one girl in a hundred who makes such a marriage has the slightest idea of what she is consenting to. I had reasons for feeling unhappy and discontented; I wanted to have a home of my own; I didn't dislike the man who said he adored me, and J thought I had done all that could possibly be required of me by telling him honestly that I was not in the least bit in love with him. It didn't take me long to discover that I had acted shamefully and that nothing on earth could ever console me or make me forgive myself. I don't mean to say that I used quite such plain language as that when I thought over my position, because there are truths to which one is almost bound in self-defence to shut one's eyes; but I knew all the time that I loathed my husband, and I knew that it would have been a thousand times better for me to have died than to have become his wife. Then, as you know, came that dreadful tragedy. I wasn't, strictly speaking, to blame for it; John hadn't the slightest reason for being jealous of poor Mr. Fraser. Yet, in a way, I was to blame; because, if I had cared for my husband, I shouldn't have wanted to escape from my thoughts by playing accompaniments for anybody. That is really the long and the short of it: you *must* care for your husband. If you don't, you will either care for somebody else, which is wicked and dishonourable, or you will make him think that you do, which is only a shade better. And when, from one or other of those causes, your home-life has become miserable, you will find horses and carriages a very poor sort of consolation.'

'They might not be much of a consolation to you,' answered Violet, who had been
more impressed by this homily than she cared
to admit; 'but I don't suppose you have
any idea of the love that I have for horses.
They quite supply the place of human beings
in my affections, and if I had a dozen of
them I should always be provided with a
dozen friends.   The most jealous husband that
ever lived would have an easy time of it with
me.   He would be welcome to forbid any other
man to cross his threshold, so long as he
allowed me to have a corner of the stables to
myself and gave orders to the stud-groom that
I wasn't to be interfered with.'

'You wouldn't talk such nonsense unless
you felt that your case was too weak for
serious argument,' remarked Ida, smiling.
'The simple truth is that you are a woman
like other women, and that you want what
every other woman wants in order to be happy.
I am not so sure about men—with them
luxuries may be a very tolerable substitute
for love—but I am quite sure about us.   I

would rather not speak of my own experience if I could help doing so; but since it can never be of any use to me now, it would perhaps be rather a pity that it should be wasted. If I am a most unhappy woman now—as I certainly am—it isn't because I have made a bad bargain, or because I have lost my husband in such a terrible way, or even because I can't forget that I am in a great measure answerable for his death. It is because of'——

'Mr. Mayne.'

It was the butler who unconsciously put this pointed and dramatic finish to a statement which might otherwise have occupied some little time; and his announcement was promptly followed by the entrance of Arthur, who shook hands with the two ladies, and, after seating himself, looked very much as if he wished that one of them would go away.

Such, at all events, was the interpretation which one of them placed upon his absent-mindedness and the difficulty which he seemed to experience in finding anything to talk about; nor was she slow to act upon what

she took for a hint. She rose presently, saying that she must give her horse a gallop
before she took him home, and in what way
she had been affected, or whether she had been
affected at all, by the half-revelation which had
been made to her Ida was unable to deter-
mine.

'That is a queer sort of girl,' Arthur Mayne
remarked, as soon as she had left the room.
'Is she a friend of yours?'

'Yes, she is a friend of mine,' answered
Ida, 'and I don't know why you call her
queer.'

'Nor do I exactly; only she strikes me as
being different from the general run of girls
somehow. She has the character of being
rather fast, you know, and—isn't she rather
hard?'

'She is neither the one nor the other; it is
you men who insist upon having hard and fast
rules, and who judge all women by them. The
only way in which I can see that she differs
from other girls is in being more independent
and more honest. Not that those qualities are

likely to benefit her much, poor child! The
chances are that she will make what is called
a good marriage—that is, a marriage into
which she would never have been led by
her personal inclinations—and then independence and honesty will be of very little service
to her.'

'Quite the reverse, I should imagine,' observed Arthur Mayne drily. 'She is going
to marry some fellow with a lot of money,
I suppose?'

'I don't know that she is; I am only
afraid of it,' answered Ida.

And then, her mind being full of the perils
which seemed to threaten Violet's future, she
proceeded to disclose to her listener somewhat
more than she was, perhaps, strictly justified
in disclosing. She abstained, it is true, from
mentioning any names; but she gave a tolerably precise and accurate account of the girl's
situation, and if Arthur Mayne had felt any
particular interest in Miss Stanton, he would
probably have had little trouble in filling up
the blanks. But, as was not unnatural, he

felt a good deal less interested in her than
in himself and his present companion; so that
his comments upon what he had been told
took a somewhat irrelevant and embarrassing
shape.

'I am very glad,' said he, 'that you have
as great a horror as I of these degrading
marriages. But indeed I was sure that you
had, and I acknowledged to myself long ago
that I had judged you unjustly. You were
the victim of—well, I dare say you will allow
me to call it a piece of sharp practice on your
father's part, and when you discovered the
truth it seemed to you too late to draw back.
You felt bound in honour to go on and to
sacrifice yourself. Yes; I can quite understand that now.'

'I was not thinking about myself,' observed
Ida rather stiffly.

'No; but I was thinking about you—I am
always thinking about you; and it does seem
to me that you have taken up altogether
wrong ideas with regard to your present circumstances. You have a way of talking as

though your life were at an end—as though
you had made a mistake which couldn't be
repaired—and that is really absurd. By the
fault of others much more than by your own,
you have had to pass through some painful
experiences ; but they are over and done with
now, and you are very little older than you
were when they began. What possible good
can you do to yourself or to anybody else
by brooding over bygones which are best forgotten ? '

Common sense, no doubt, was on the side
of the querist ; but perhaps common sense
was not exactly what Ida required of him, and
certainly she did not care to be favoured with
his advice. 'I shall do very well, thank you,'
answered she in a tone of voice which was intended to preclude further argument. 'As a
matter of fact I am not much given to brooding ; but, if I were, I should have occupations
enough to prevent me from indulging my
morbid tastes. Which reminds me, by the
bye, that I ought to be looking up some of
my poor people at this moment.'

Arthur humbly got up and took his leave.
He understood that he had been snubbed and
thought that he had very likely deserved a
snubbing : he was too modest to conjecture
that Ida might have been more merciful if he
had been a little more explicit, as well as a
little less eager to declare that he cherished
no grudge against her for her treatment of him
in the past.   And profoundly surprised would
he have been had it been revealed to him
that his prompt departure caused her to shed
a few tears of grief and mortification.

Most of us are apt to believe that a revela-
tion of our neighbours' true thoughts and
feelings would be worth almost any money ;
and so perhaps it would be, provided that it
did not last too long.   Yet it may be surmised that the course of life and this world
would be rendered insupportably dull by any
permanent curtailment of the play of imagina-
tion, and assuredly such a doubtful boon would
have deprived Violet Stanton, as she rode
homewards that afternoon, of the pleasure of
exercising her brain with speculations which

she found extremely interesting. Mrs. Chaine's confession and appeal had not been without effect upon her; at the bottom of her heart she could not help knowing that her friend was right, and that the absence of love cannot really be atoned for by the substitution of material enjoyments; but at the same time she was fully alive to the fact that Ida was not situated as she was. After all, was not love a luxury, like other luxuries, which some people can afford, while others can't? Ida could afford that luxury nowadays, and it looked very much as if she had whistled back her former lover on the earliest available opportunity. That might be a very coarse and uncharitable way of putting things; but wasn't it the truth?

Now, if Ida had been a maiden instead of a widow, if she had had no income of her own, and (what was even more to the purpose) no lover, she might possibly have held less exalted views upon the subject of matrimony.

'Besides,' mused Violet, 'she isn't a bit like me; she is much more of a woman than I am;

she wants all sorts of things that I don't care a
straw about; and she doesn't hunt. Hunting
makes all the difference. I have never been in
love, and I don't believe I shall ever meet a
man worth falling in love with. If I had been
idiot enough to lose my heart to anybody, that
would be another matter; but since I haven't,
and since it seems to be necessary that I should
marry, I might as well take Sir Harvey, who
says he has lost his heart to me, and who
knows that he will have to provide me with
horses if he wants to keep me in good humour.'

Violet arrived simultaneously at that logical
conclusion and at the outskirts of St. Albyn's.
Now, it was upon the outskirts of St. Albyn's
that the cavalry barracks were situated, and
therefore there was nothing surprising in the
circumstance that she presently encountered a
young man who wore one arm in a sling and
who made use of the other to take off his hat
to her. The circumstance was not surprising,
nor had she any idea of allowing herself to be
disconcerted by it.

'How do you do? I am glad to see you

walking about again,' she called out, without drawing rein.

But apparently he took it for granted that she did not mean to pass him by in that off-hand fashion; for he placed himself full in her path, insomuch that she was compelled to check her horse.

'Is that the hunter?' he asked.

'That,' replied Violet, to whom his scrutinising glance presented itself at once in the light of an impertinence, 'is the hunter. Anything obviously wrong with him?'

'No—oh, no; a very good, useful sort of animal, I should say. What about that off fore-leg, though? Isn't there——?'

'Certainly not; nothing of the kind. Oh, well, of course he has been fired—any fool could see that; but if you can discover a splint or a spavin in any one of Bob's four legs, I'll sell him to you for five pounds on the spot. Now then!'

That impudent young man actually passed his hand over each of the horse's legs; after which he coolly made him pick them up and examined his feet. Then he grinned and said, 'All right, Miss Stanton; we can pass him. I suppose he knows how to jump—in a humble way?'

'Now look here,' said Violet; 'I'll undertake to say that this horse could lift you—or two of you, for that matter—over the very biggest fence in the country. Of course I don't promise that he *would* do it, because, if you were on his back, you would very likely play the idiot and interfere with him, as nine men out of ten do with their horses; but just you come out with us this season and see whether it doesn't take you all your time to follow him, that's all!'

'I thought I should get a rise out of you,' remarked Hubert complacently.

'Oh, you did, did you? Well, I congratulate you on your success. You are a nice, civil-spoken sort of family, I must say! I have just been to see your sister-in-law, who has favoured me with a long lecture which I thought rather uncalled-for. Kindly meant, though, no doubt.'

'A lecture?—upon what subject?' inquired Hubert.

'Oh, upon the subject of general deportment and behaviour, I believe. It didn't interest me particularly, and I don't suppose it would interest you. I have the vanity, you see, to imagine that I am the best judge of my own affairs. Good evening.'

She gave a shake to her reins and moved on, so that Hubert was forced to stand aside; but she had not moved forward many paces when he caught her up and said penitently: 'I haven't offended you, have I? It was only chaff, you know, about the horse. He's really as nice-looking a little horse as I've seen for— for I don't know how long, and I'm sure he must carry you splendidly. And—and, Miss Stanton, I hope you are not angry with Ida. She may have been cheeky; but she can't have meant to be cheeky; because I can assure you that you haven't a more sincere friend and admirer in the world than she is.'

Who could resist so touching an appeal?

Violet laughed heartily and answered: 'Don't be alarmed. Mrs. Chaine isn't half as cheeky as you are, and if she were I should be generous enough to forgive her. Only don't criticise Bob again, please, because I don't like it.'

She continued to laugh softly to herself for some little time after she had left him. He was only a boy, and his conduct was most distinctly and innocently boyish; yet, if one must needs draw comparisons (and how is one to help doing so?) there is no denying that boys are pleasanter specimens of the human race than old men. It doesn't necessarily follow that one would rather marry an impecunious boy than a well-to-do old man; still it is permissible to regret that the wrong people should be so frequently found in the right place.

Notwithstanding this legitimate cause for dissatisfaction with an ill-ordered world, Violet was in pretty good spirits when she entered her mother's drawing-room, where Mrs. Stanton had been eagerly awaiting her return for more than an hour.

'Oh, here you are at last!' the good lady exclaimed. 'Who do you think called this afternoon and waited for ever so long in hopes of seeing you?—Sir Harvey Amherst!'

Violet's face fell as she sank into an armchair. 'I have indeed missed a treat,' she observed gloomily. 'Is he likely to call again soon?'

'Of course he is; he told me frankly that he had come to St. Albyn's for that especial purpose. He is staying at the White Hart, and he has promised to lunch with us to-morrow. Oh, Violet dear, I am so very, very glad!'

'H'm! so am I,' answered Violet; 'I'm quite overjoyed; I hardly know how to contain myself. Isn't it about time to go and dress for dinner?'

CHAPTER XXVIII

AN UNREASONABLE REASON

VIOLET'S rest was a good deal disturbed that
night, and when she rose the next morning she
was even more uneasy and unhappy than she
had been on retiring to bed. The coming day
must inevitably witness her decision as to her
future lot, and the worst of it was that she felt
quite unable to come to a decision. Somehow
or other, that brief and very unsentimental
parley which she had held with Hubert Chaine
had influenced her more powerfully than all
Ida's advice and experience. She was conscious
of this and rather surprised that it should be so;
because, after all, she was not enamoured of the
young man, nor, if she had been, could she
have dreamt of espousing a pauper : perhaps it
was the mere fact of his youth, which had
chanced to touch a sympathetic chord in her

heart, and had thus rendered her more alive to the impossibility of any sympathetic association between Sir Harvey Amherst and herself. Well, it was open to her to refuse Sir Harvey —only she was quite sure that, if she did, she would repent of her folly immediately afterwards. Thus she wavered and debated throughout the morning, and, when the dreaded luncheon hour drew near, was fain to cast herself upon the guidance of circumstances, after the immemorial fashion of those who cannot make up their own minds.

Sir Harvey made his appearance punctually, and it was not a little provoking to notice how cheerful and confident he looked. It even struck Violet that he wore a certain air of quiet self-approval, as who should say, 'Here I am, you see, true to my word. I need not tell you that I might make a far more magnificent alliance than this, if I chose; but no! I abide by my choice, which I see no present reason to regret. And an uncommonly lucky young woman you are to have been chosen by me!'

No such speech, nor any such thought, was in poor Sir Harvey's mind, although it must be owned that his manner was scarcely that of a diffident suitor. Why, indeed, should it be? He argued, reasonably enough, that he would not have been invited to luncheon unless a favourable answer had been in store for him; Mrs. Stanton had spoken on the previous afternoon as though everything were settled, and his chief anxiety for the moment was to keep up conversation under conditions which could not but be a trifle embarrassing. During luncheon, therefore, he was as voluble and as entertaining as he could manage to be, relating such scraps of social gossip as seemed likely to be intelligible to his hearers, dwelling (for Violet's benefit) upon the performances of the best two-year-olds of the season, and generally doing his best to relieve the situation of awkwardness. He met with little assistance from either of the ladies; for Mrs. Stanton was preoccupied with fears lest the cook should be guilty of some atrocity, while Violet was still young enough to be in-

capable of opening her lips when disinclined
to talk.

'I suppose you are not going to stay in St.
Albyn's after to-day, are you?' was almost the
only remark which she addressed directly to
him, and it could not be called exactly a
happy one.

Sir Harvey looked down and smiled, and
replied that that must depend. He could not
very well have said anything else; but naturally this question and answer brought about
a rather uncomfortable interval of silence.
However, he speedily recovered himself; and
as he protested that he never touched sweets in
the middle of the day (meaning, perhaps, that
he was not in the habit of eating solid *soufflés*
or gelatinous jellies at any hour), it was not
very long before he was relieved from further
exertions.

And now came the question of how he was
to secure the five minutes' private conversation
with Violet which it had been the object of his
visit to obtain. After having followed the
ladies upstairs, he was thinking of asking her

whether she would take him to inspect her horse, when Mrs. Stanton earned his gratitude and displayed her own good sense by simply quitting the room, without excuse or apology. Violet was left standing beside the open window, and if she could have jumped out of it under any less penalty than breaking her bones, it is not at all unlikely that she would have adopted that futile and undignified method of escape. Escape by that or by any other means being impossible, she turned round to find Destiny at her elbow, in the shape of an elderly gentleman of winning manners and fashionable exterior.

'At last!' he exclaimed. 'If you only knew how I have longed for this moment to come! But I told you I would be patient, and I think I may claim to have kept my promise.'

'I suppose you couldn't contrive to be patient a little longer, could you?' asked Violet, ignobly clutching at a straw.

'My dear Miss Stanton, do you think it would be quite fair to impose a second period

of exile upon me? And really—would there be
any use in doing so? Surely you must know
by this time whether it is in your power to
make me happy or not, and surely you must
see that it would be needlessly cruel to keep
me any longer in suspense.'

'You seem to take it for granted that I
mean to accept you,' was Violet's resentful and
somewhat irrelevant rejoinder.

'No, indeed!—how could I take that for
granted when you have as good as refused me
once? All I do take for granted is that you
have done me the justice to remember my
hopes and think over them all this time, and
that you are too merciful to torture a fellow-
creature unnecessarily.'

'Oh, torture is a very big word; I don't
think there is much danger of your being
put to torture by anything that I may say
or do.'

Sir Harvey laughed. 'I don't want to use
big words,' he answered; 'I don't like them,
and I always try to avoid them. Still, in
sober earnest, suspense *is* torture; and, if you

will pardon my saying so, I can't help suspecting that you would be almost as glad as I should to be relieved from it.'

'That is true enough,' observed Violet.

She was silent for a moment, biting her lips and looking down. Then she suddenly raised her eyes and said: 'I can't understand your wishing to marry a girl who doesn't love you! It is so evident that, if she consents, you must have the worst of the bargain! You can offer me all sorts of pleasant things; but what in the world have I to offer you?'

'My dear,' replied Sir Harvey, drawing a step nearer and taking her hand, 'you can give me yourself. Are you so modest that you don't think yourself worth more than all the pleasant things that money can purchase?'

There may have been some lack of delicacy in his words; yet they represented the proposed contract in no other light than that in which Violet had always contemplated it, and it is difficult to say why she should have been so forcibly repelled by them. She snatched her hand away and said quickly: 'If I am not modest, I am sure I ought to be! It doesn't make one feel particularly proud to think that one has been upon the point of agreeing to dispose of one's self in return for a good big supply of those pleasant things. And the ugliest part of it is that I should really like to make the agreement even now, if I could. Happily for you — and happily for me, too, I daresay—I can't. You will have to marry somebody else, Sir Harvey; and if it consoles you at all to know that I am sincerely sorry for it, I make you a present of that consolation.'

Sir Harvey was rather taken aback; but he did not strike his colours. 'I am sure you are speaking upon the impulse of the moment,' said he; 'something has upset you or put you out; isn't it so? I can't believe that you would have let me come here to-day if you had been determined to reject me.'

'Haven't I just said that I was upon the very verge of accepting you? That is just what makes it so certain that I never shall now. Did you ever want very much to tell a lie and then find that, somehow or other, you couldn't for the life of you help telling the truth? If you have, you will understand exactly how I feel.'

Probably Sir Harvey did not understand exactly how she felt; for he said, in a tone of gentle remonstrance, 'But nobody is asking or expecting you to tell a lie. You were quite open and honest with me in London, and I admired you for it. I should be very sorry if you condescended to be anything else.'

'Oh, I am capable of a great deal in the way of condescension,' answered the girl, half laughing; 'I only meant to say that there are some things of which one isn't capable when it comes to the push—though why one shouldn't be I'm sure I don't know.'

Sir Harvey endeavoured to reason with her. He dwelt upon the purely fanciful nature of a reluctance which she herself was unable to explain; he promised to demand no more from her than she could give; he professed to be perfectly conscious of all that was implied in

the disparity between their ages; finally, he
ventured to hint that she was throwing away
one of those golden opportunities upon a
recurrence of which no mortal can safely
count. But his eloquence and his patience
were alike wasted.

'It is useless to go on talking,' Violet,
whose patience was more easily exhausted than
his, said at last; 'if we were to argue until
this time to-morrow I should only have the
same stupid answer to make—I can't do it.
Of course I am sorry if this is a disappointment
to you; but it won't be a very severe one, will
it? I mean, there are such a number of girls
who would be delighted to replace me, and
who will suit you quite as well as I should
have done. With your advantages you have
only to go in and win.'

That was, perhaps, true: moreover, it was
beginning to dawn upon this elderly and
slightly aggrieved suitor that, although common sense may be an excellent foundation for
contentment in married life, a trifling flavour
of romance is not altogether out of place in the

young. He could not resist saying, 'Upon my word, Miss Stanton, you are quite the most unromantic young lady I have ever met with in all my life.'

'I have always, until to-day, believed myself to be singularly free from nonsense of any kind,' responded Violet; 'but it strikes me that this present proceeding of mine is about as near an approach to romance as I am likely to achieve. Well, it can't be helped! We shall part friends, I hope.'

Sir Harvey felt that something in the shape of an apology might have been considered his due; but he was a gentleman; he was kind-hearted and easy-going, and, for choice, he preferred to be friends with everybody. So he said:

'Oh yes; why not? Naturally, I am sorry, and you won't wonder at my being a little puzzled into the bargain; but I have no right to complain or to think myself ill-used. You may be sure, my dear Miss Stanton, that if ever I can serve you in any way——'

'Well, to tell you the truth, you can,'

interrupted Violet, with scant ceremony; 'there is one thing that you can do for me, and I should be sincerely grateful to you if you would do it. It is to go away before my mother comes back. She isn't the best hand in the world at controlling her feelings, and if she were to bounce in upon us—as she may do at any moment—and hear what I have been about during her absence, we might have a painful scene.'

Sir Harvey jumped up with alacrity and with a somewhat alarmed look. He would have been out of the room in two seconds if it had not suddenly occurred to him that such a precipitate flight might be a little bit cowardly.

' I—I'll see you through, if you like,' said he heroically. ' I know what these old women are when they're roused, and I am willing to take the whole blame upon myself. When all's said and done, she can't eat me.'

For the very first time in the course of Violet's acquaintanceship with him he presented a genuine appearance of youth; and indeed it is quite true that nine-tenths of us remain boys even after we have become old boys, whereas old girls—but everybody of ripe years has had sad reason to find out what sort of a person an old girl is.   Violet burst into a hearty laugh ; though, for some reason or other, the tears were not far away from her eyes.

'Thank you very much,' said she ; 'you have plenty of pluck and more generosity than ought to be thrown away upon the likes of me. But I really don't stand in need of support ; my poor old mother isn't a virago, and all she will do will be to weep copiously.   I only thought it would be rather better for you to be out of the way before the flood-gates were opened.'

Sir Harvey so obviously concurred in this view that it was an easy matter to get rid of him.   After a few more hurried assurances of his unalterable affection and esteem he stole softly down the stairs ; and no sooner had the front door closed behind him with a bang than Mrs. Stanton, who may have been waiting for that signal, trotted into the room with a coun-

tenance expressive of the tenderest and most
joyous sympathy.

Well, nobody can be expected to feel much
sympathy with match-making mammas, who,
nevertheless, are fellow-creatures of like (or
something like) passions with ourselves, and
whose sorrows are probably not less keen,
although they may be less legitimate, than
our own. A few spare grains of pity may
surely be bestowed upon Mrs. Stanton by the
magnanimous, seeing that it was not she
who had thrown her daughter at Sir Harvey
Amherst's head, and that she was utterly
unprepared for the blow which awaited her.
She fulfilled Violet's prediction by weeping
piteously ; but she managed, between her
sobs, to give evidence of rather more acute-
ness than the rejected baronet had displayed,
inasmuch as she exclaimed :

'It is childish and ridiculous to pretend
that you have behaved in this extraordinary
way without any reason, Violet! There *must*
be a reason, and all I can say is, I do hope and
trust it may not be a terribly bad one! You

know as well as I do that I couldn't possibly
sanction your engagement to any one beneath
you in rank, or destitute of sufficient income,
so you needn't ask me to do such a thing.'

'Why cry out before you are hurt?'
returned Violet. 'I haven't plighted my
troth to the livery stable-keeper or to the
youngest lieutenant in the new hussar regiment, and I don't propose to do so. I propose
to be an old maid ; it seems to me that that is
the part for which I have been cut out by
Nature.'

'Very well, my dear,' said Mrs. Stanton,
sitting up and drying her eyes; 'when your
mother is no longer with you, you will perhaps be sorry for having treated her so heart-
lessly.'

But Violet did not think it likely that her
remorse, if she ever came to feel any, would
take that particular form.

CHAPTER XXIX

TWO HALF CONFESSIONS

THE most exasperating as well as the most hopelessly irreconcilable people in the world are those who nurse their real or imaginary grievances, while flattering themselves that they have forgiven the unlucky individuals who have chanced to aggrieve them. To this class, roughly speaking, belong clerics of all denominations and the immense majority of women. The ordinary human being cannot cope with them, should not try to reason with them, and will fail ignominiously if he or she be so ill-advised as to attempt to bring home to them any sense of the illogical absurdity of their attitude. The ordinary human being would, of course, like either to fight or to be friends; but the ordinary human being must reckon with the exceptional members of his race, who, after all, are very numerous, and must submit, every now and then, to be half pardoned for sins which he has not committed, since no other course is open to him.

Violet Stanton had not, it will be allowed, sinned against her mother by refusing Sir Harvey Amherst. She had dutifully announced the fact that he had proposed to her; she had honestly stated that she was as yet uncertain whether she could accept him or not, and her ultimate inability to do so could not fairly be counted as an offence against anybody but herself and, possibly, the rejected one. All this Mrs. Stanton admitted; she said in so many words that she had no right to complain, and did not complain; yet she absolutely refused to be comforted. She had a right—or at all events she thought she had—to sigh and weep all day long; she had a right to deplore the folly and caprice of one whose happiness was much dearer to her than her own; she had a right, in short, to make herself thoroughly disagreeable, and of this she took full advantage.

Violet, conscious of having behaved foolishly, endeavoured to be patient, and succeeded about as well as any girl in her place could have been expected to succeed; still every-day life was not rendered pleasant for her at this time, and she very naturally began to cast about elsewhere for the sympathy which she could not hope to obtain at home.

She obtained it, and plenty of it, at the White House, whither she took herself and a recital of her sorrows a few days after Sir Harvey's departure, and where both met with a warm welcome.

'I can't tell you how rejoiced I am!' cried Ida. 'I am ashamed of myself for having ever doubted you; but I confess that I did doubt you a little, and it was partly your own fault, because you would persist in pretending to be so worldly and heartless. What a relief it is to know that you have resisted a temptation which ought really to have been no temptation at all! Don't you yourself feel it to be a relief?'

'Not the least bit in the world,' answered
Violet; 'I only feel that I haven't had the
courage of my opinions, and that now I shall
be punished in fifty ways for my cowardice.
A nicer old gentleman than Sir Harvey
Amherst I never shall meet again—nor a
richer old gentleman—nor, in all probability,
another who will offer to share his riches with
me. Virtue must be its own reward; for I
know full well that I shall get nothing else in
the way of compensation.'

'Oh, you will get your reward in due
season,' said Ida, smiling and nodding at her
confidently; 'I will make so bold as to pre-
dict that much, and some day you will admit
that I have been a true prophet. And don't
you bother your head about your mother's
disappointment. Mothers are always disappointed when these *contretemps* occur;
but that is only because they have forgotten
how they themselves felt when they were
young, and because they don't realise that
luxuries which have become essential to them
are not at all essential to their juniors. You

may depend upon it that you will very soon
live that trouble down.'

'H'm!' returned Violet, who knew her
mother rather better than Mrs. Chaine did.
'Well, to be sure, the hunting will begin
before long; and that, as you know, means
being out all day and going to bed immediately after dinner. If only I had a
second horse I daresay I might manage to
pull through; but if I can get two days a
week out of Bob, that will be the very outside that I ought to ask of him, and hiring is
expensive work.'

'We must see what we can do for you on
the off days,' said her friend. 'Does polo go
on during the winter? I should think it
would; and anyhow, an asylum will always
be open to you here. I really don't think
there is any need for you to tremble at the
prospect of the future.'

Considering what Ida's hopes and intentions with reference to the future were,
this was a tolerably bold assertion; but
Violet, having no suspicion of these, felt

comforted, and expressed herself to that
effect.

'I don't care much about looking on at
polo,' said she; 'it is a stupid sort of game
for everybody except the players, I think.
But I should be grateful if I might be allowed
to come and see you when I have no other
excuse for leaving home. My mother and I
are very fond of each other in a way, only we
never seem quite to hit it off together somehow, and I shouldn't mind telling you lots of
things that I could never dream of telling
her.'

Ida thought that sounded very like the
overture to a confession; but whether it was
intended as such or not she was unable to
discover, for before she had time to make
any response the door was thrown open,
admitting Wilfrid Chaine, who, after he had
shaken hands with the two ladies, announced
that he had returned on the previous evening
with a view to spending the coming winter at
home. He appeared to be in capital spirits;
he was full of the improvements which he had

carried out or proposed to carry out at Chaine
Court, and he addressed his remarks chiefly to
Miss Stanton, who, to tell the truth, was not
wholly insensible of the compliment thus paid
to her.

' Have you provided yourself with a good
string of hunters ? ' she asked. Because that
naturally struck her as being the first duty
of a man in his position.

' I have bought some horses, and I have
paid good prices for them,' he answered,
laughing. 'More than that I mustn't venture
to say to such a competent critic. You will
have to tell me later on whether I have been
swindled or not.'

' You won't have been swindled if you have
gone to the right people and paid the right
money,' Violet assured him gravely. 'It's
quite a mistake to imagine that horse-dealers
are greater swindlers than other tradesmen ;
they know just as well as other tradesmen
know that honesty pays in the long-run.
Only, of course, the man who buys of them
mustn't be a born fool. I mean, he must

have some sort of notion of what a hunter ought to be, and some notion of how to ride him when he has got him.'

Wilfrid, with an amused smile, said he hoped he was not altogether devoid of knowledge upon those essential points. 'Still,' he added, 'at the risk of incurring your contempt, I must own that I don't think chasing a fox the one and only thing worth living for. I have two or three spare strings to my bow— and so, I rather suspect, have you.'

Violet shook her head. 'With me,' she replied, 'it is hunting first and other pursuits nowhere. I *can* ride; but I can't do anything else decently, so what's the use of trying? I'm not bragging about it, you know — quite the contrary. I'm rather ashamed of having such limited capacities as it is, and I should be ten times more ashamed if I were a man. Every man ought to be able to ride; but then he ought to be able to distinguish himself in many other ways besides—in Parliament, for instance, provided that he has the means. By the way, you are going to be an M.P., aren't you?'

'That will have to depend upon whether I can find a constituency to return me. Yes; I am in hopes of entering Parliament some fine day—as a modern Conservative. Are you a modern Conservative, Miss Stanton? Or are you too modern to be anything but an out-and-out Radical?'

'As far as I know myself,' replied Violet, 'I am an old-fashioned Tory.'

'Ah, that is just what I should like to be, if I dared; but it doesn't do to be too daring in these degenerate days. What are your views with regard to free education, for example?'

Violet declined to commit herself upon matters of detail. Broadly stated, her principles, she said, were those of England's greatest ministers; she was all for maintaining the honour of the country abroad and order at home; she considered that the Constitution, as it stood, was good enough for all law-abiding people, and she was

strongly of opinion that any tampering with
the game-laws ought to be resisted.

She allowed herself to be drawn by degrees
into a discussion which greatly entertained
Wilfrid, and in the course of which he found
her quite charming. She talked a good deal
of nonsense, of course; but he did not mind
that: according to his notions, women were
never sent into this world for the purpose of
talking sense. Their mission, he conceived,
was to be wives and mothers eventually, and
to be as pretty and agreeable as they could in
the meantime. It was because Violet was
both pretty and agreeable that he felt disposed to lend a kindly hand towards the
fulfilment of her destiny. He was not in
love—he had burnt his fingers once at that
game and had no intention of losing control
over himself a second time—still, before he
brought his visit to a close, he was in a state
quite as nearly approaching thereto as was
at all safe. He had taken care to inquire
casually after Sir Harvey Amherst, had
learnt that the sprightly baronet had just

been spending a couple of days in St. Albyn's, and had rightly concluded from the tone in which this information was imparted to him that his most formidable rival had been dismissed. From that circumstance he drew deductions which may not have been justifiable, but which, upon the face of them, were highly plausible ; so that he walked home in the best of good humours.

Ida, who had taken little part in the conversation, had listened to it, and had noticed Wilfrid's attentions without any disquietude. She had felt sure all along that he would sooner or later offer his hand and heart to her young friend, and she now felt sure that her young friend would unhesitatingly refuse him. There could, indeed, be no room for hesitation in his case ; because, although he was younger than Sir Harvey Amherst, he was not nearly as rich, and the same reason which had led Violet to turn reluctantly away from her wealthier suitor must be equally operative as regarded him. By all means, then, let him try his luck ; and when he, too, should have been forced to stand aside, it would be time for Hubert to make his modest effort. Meanwhile, since there was nothing whatsoever to be gained by outspoken depreciation of a man whom she cordially disliked, she abstained from any criticisms upon Wilfrid, and endeavoured to take the conversation up at the point where it had been interrupted by his entrance.

'Now that we are alone again,' she began, 'perhaps you will deliver yourself of some of the "lots of things" that you don't like to say to your mother. I daresay I might contrive to guess what one or two of them are.'

But Violet was no longer in the mood to be expansive. 'Oh,' she answered, 'I wasn't thinking of anything in particular; I only meant to say that I shouldn't be afraid of being misunderstood if I let you hear my impressions of events and people just as they occurred to me. Mr. Wilfrid Chaine is an instance. I don't mind telling you that I thought him a very good sort of fellow this afternoon—though I never thought him so before—and that I should like to see more of him; but I couldn't say that to my mother without convincing her upon the spot that I wanted to marry him or that he wanted to marry me, and in about a month's time she would be prepared to swear that I had led her to believe as much. You see, it is simply incredible to her that any woman in the world would remain an old maid from choice.'

'I don't think you will be an old maid,' observed Ida, smiling; 'but I certainly don't think you will ever marry Wilfrid. And I should be very sorry indeed if I did think so.'

Violet shrugged her shoulders as she rose. 'There doesn't seem to be much probability of my bringing sorrow upon you in that way,' said she. 'As for spinsterhood, it has its advantages; and if any benevolent old gentleman or lady would leave me a thousand a year, a spinster I should undoubtedly live and die. Well, it is time for me to be off

now; I shall come and inflict myself upon
you again as soon as I get another fit of the
blues.'

Ida herself was occasionally afflicted in
that way, and was accustomed, at such times,
to seek an antidote in those visits to the poor
which had caused the vicar of the parish and
the Fraser girls to speak so highly of her.
When Violet left her she found that she had
a spare hour and a half before dinner and
remembered that she had promised to look
up a certain retainer of the Fraser family, on
whose behalf her interest had been bespoken,
but who had hitherto met her advances with
surly ingratitude.   This was no other than
Barton, the gamekeeper, whose differences
with the late owner of Hatton Park had, as
may be remembered, resulted in his dismissal.
To Barton Leonard Fraser's sudden death had
been a piece of good luck, of which he could
hardly be blamed for having taken advantage.
He had, at all events, done so, inasmuch as
he had not deemed it incumbent upon him
to acquaint his new master with the fact

that he had been dismissed, and, like the other servants, he had been allowed to retain his situation. However, he had not dis-; charged his duties long when he fell ill, and he was now believed to be in a hopeless condition. Colonel Fraser had behaved very kindly to the man, engaging a substitute in his place, but refusing to turn him out of his cottage or to stop his wages; so that he really stood in no need of the benevolence of Mrs. Chaine, to whom, as has been said, he had given a decidedly unfriendly welcome on previous occasions.

Nevertheless, he seemed glad to see her this time and declared that he was so. She found him sitting, propped up by pillows, in his armchair, a gaunt, emaciated figure, with deep lines of suffering about his mouth and round his sunken eyes. He breathed with difficulty and spoke in a hoarse, broken voice.

'I should ha' had to send for you without you'd come, m'm,' said he; 'I've got summat to tell you afore I die—that is, if I'm agoin' to die, as they tell me I am.'

He glanced round at his wife, who was standing behind his chair, and impatiently waved her away.

'Time for you to go out and feed them chicken, 'Liza,' said he; 'work's got to be done, whether there's life or death in the house.'

And when the woman had submissively retired he bent forward and whispered eagerly: 'Is it death, m'm? I said they'd told me so; but they won't tell me, nor yet I can't be sure —though I b'lieve as 'tis.'

Ida hesitated. She knew that the man was suffering from an aneurism which must kill him eventually and might kill him at any moment; but she shrank from taking upon herself a responsibility which the doctor had apparently evaded.

'I am afraid you are very ill, Barton,' she said at length, 'and of course you are aware that you may never be any better. I think, if I were you, I would ask the doctor to tell me the truth. But if you have anything upon your mind, I am sure you would feel easier for having got rid of it. You may rely upon

my keeping any secret that you may choose
to confide to me.'

Barton shook his head, with the ghost of
a smile. '"Tisn't that sort o' secret,' he
replied. 'Once you know, m'm, everybody
'll know—that's for sartain. But it ain't
agoin' to be told to you not without I'm as
good as in my coffin. For why? 'Cause we
can't bring the dead back to life, and 'cause I
won't bring no man to the gallows—that's
why. Poor Mr. John he's dead and gone, 't
won't make no odds to him now whether the
truth is let out or kep' dark; but 'twill
make a precious sight of difference to the
one as did the job, do you see, m'm. That's
where 'tis.'

'Do you mean that my husband never
killed Mr. Fraser, and that you knew it all
along?' exclaimed Ida.

Barton nodded. 'More 'n that, I knew
who done it. More 'n that again, Mr. Wilfrid
must ha' known very well as his brother were
innocent. Oh, I ain't the only one as has
kep' his mouth shut, nor yet the only one

as has had reasons for keepin' of his mouth shut.'

'You have acted very wickedly and very cruelly,' said Ida, with white cheeks and dilated eyes; 'but though it is too late now to undo what you have done, you can at least make some sort of reparation by clearing an innocent man's memory. Who was the murderer?—I insist upon knowing!'

In her excitement she seized the sick man's wrist and gripped it violently; but he only gazed at her in silence, with a wistful, suffering look, which gradually changed to one of dull obstinacy.

'I shan't say no more now,' he answered at last. 'No later 'n this mornin' I thought 'twas all over with me; but I've picked up a bit and I may be gettin' the better of this here disease for aught I know. When I'm at the point of death, m'm, I'll send for you, and you shall hear all about it. You'll understand then what my motives was for not speaking no sooner.'

'I understand already that they must be

bad motives,' returned Ida. 'Y_____ _e admitted that you know who the _____ _rer was, and after that you are boun_ ___mit more. In fact, I should think yo___ _ht be forced to admit more.'

But Barton rejoined stolidly t___ __ didn't know who could force him to speak, adding that, if force were attempted, the truth should never be revealed by him. He was equally obdurate when Ida represented to him that his behaviour was cruel to her, treacherous to the dead, and dangerous to his own soul's welfare.

'I has my reasons, same as Mr. Wilfrid Chaine had his,' the man replied. 'If I'm to die, I'll make a clean breast of it; but if I'm to live, I'll hold my tongue, whether 'tis right or whether 'tis wrong.'

From that determination he was not to be moved, and all that Ida could obtain from him before she left his side was a repetition of his promise that he would send for her the moment that his condition should be pronounced incurable. Her mind, as she walked

as in a tumult of mixed and con-
flic notions. Poor John had really been
gui hen, of the crime for which he had
been eavily punished! She thought of
his ba ment, of his deprivation of all that
could ha made life worth having to him, of
his lonely and miserable death, and a sharp
pang of pain. and remorse contracted her
heart-strings. But then, why had he run
away? Who could the actual culprit have
been? Not Barton himself? Not—surely
not—Wilfrid? She did not know what to
think; and the more she puzzled her brains
over it the more vague did her conjectures
become. But through them all, and mingled
with the musings which kept her awake
during the greater part of the night, there
ran an undercurrent of rejoicing that was
not, perhaps, wholly unselfish — for, alas!
which of us is wholly unselfish, or can even
pretend to be so? To be the widow of a
murderer is a terrible position; it is one
which is, or ought to be, incompatible with
any position save that of perpetual widow-

hood. But to be the widow of a man who has only been singularly unfortunate—well, that does not imply quite the same restrictions. This was what Ida was thinking, though she was unconscious of entertaining any such thoughts; because she felt as convinced as it was possible to be that Arthur Mayne would never again ask her to be his wife. Meanwhile, it was her very evident duty to see the doctor and impress upon him that the dying man ought no longer to be kept in ignorance of his state. What if he should expire suddenly and his secret should perish with him? She had heard that people afflicted with the disease from which he suffered usually do die in that way.

CHAPTER XXX

A FOOLISH BUSINESS

IT may be safely affirmed that in order to
enjoy cub-hunting one must be very young
— or else, perhaps, a huntsman. Certain
Masters of Foxhounds profess to delight in
that form of sport, and one who has never
occupied, nor ever will occupy, their proud
position ought, no doubt, to repose faith in
the sincerity of their statements. Still it
is not very easy for a middle-aged man to
believe that other middle-aged men can really
like getting out of bed before daylight for
the purpose of galloping across country in a
sweltering heat.

Youth, however, is a sufficient explanation
of all kinds of otherwise inexplicable conduct,
and Violet Stanton no more objected to a
curtailment of her night's rest than she did

to saddling and bridling her own horse. Both of these things she did, one still, dewy morning, and both produced upon her an effect of profound satisfaction. As she rode through the silent streets of St. Albyn's, Bob's hoofs rousing the sleeping echoes and perhaps also causing some sleepy citizens to turn round and wonder drowsily who could be abroad at such an hour, she tasted something of the joys of independence and irresponsibility which, after all, must be acknowledged to be very real joys, although most of us can hardly hope to make acquaintance with them, save through instinct and analogy. She was going to be happy for several hours; she was going to see the hounds again; she was going to feel her good little horse bound under her with an excitement in which she could so thoroughly participate; she had given due notice of the fact that she might not be able to get back in time for luncheon, and for the present she had nothing and nobody to think about except herself. Certainly she did not mean to think about Sir Harvey Amherst,

whose agreeable manners and glittering pro-
posals must now be consigned to the lumber-
room of the past, and of whom, weighing one
consideration against another, she was truly
thankful to be rid. Still less was she disposed to waste time in wondering whether a
crippled lieutenant of hussars would, notwithstanding his disabled condition, put in an
appearance at a meet eight miles away from
barracks. She wanted no lieutenants of hussars nor any elderly baronets on that delicious,
cool morning: what she wanted was a good
gallop; and, from information which she had
received, she thought it quite likely that she
would get one.

Therefore, when she reached Shamford Mill
and joined a very small and select group of
horsemen, it was a matter of little consequence
to her that one of these, who wore his right
arm in a sling, should approach her, with a
bow and a radiant smile, saying: 'I'm so
awfully glad you have turned up; I was
afraid this would be a bit too early for
you.'

'No fear!' she rejoined somewhat disdainfully; 'it isn't early hours that can keep me at home when hounds are running. I should have thought you were hardly fit to ride yet, though.'

'Oh, I'm all right,' Hubert answered. 'I'm minus an arm for the time being; but that don't matter with a sensible old gee like the one I'm on. Besides, I don't suppose there's much chance of our having a run.'

'We shall have a run if we find,' returned Violet confidently, 'and we're pretty sure to find; I'll answer for that. As for jumping— well, since you have only one arm, perhaps your best plan would be to follow me until I hold up my hand. Then you won't come to grief.'

The young man thanked her warmly and quite humbly. 'It is such an age since I rode over this country that I have clean forgotten all about it,' said he, 'and I am sure, from all I have heard, that, even if I were perfectly sound, I couldn't do better than take you for a pilot—as you are kind enough to let me do so. You needn't be afraid of my riding in your pocket.'

'He seemed, indeed, to be sincerely as well as modestly desirous of re-establishing himself in the good graces of a lady whom he had presumed to chaff when they had last met; and Violet, recognising and approving of this change in his demeanour, was graciously pleased to favour him with a few valuable hints.

But when her prophecy had been fulfilled, and when they had got well away upon a burning scent, it was not upon Hubert Chaine or upon any other man in the wide world that she had leisure to bestow much thought. She did, indeed, remember him when she reached a bank on the farther side of which, as she knew, there were posts and rails, and she threw up her hand by way of warning; but after Bob, with his customary cleverness, had lifted her safely across that obstacle she did not turn her head, presuming that it would have proved too hard a nut for outsiders and disabled horse-men to crack. As a matter of fact, it did dispose of the majority of the field, and for another glorious and happy ten minutes she had the joy of racing over pasture lands, with nobody near her except the Master and the huntsman. Then a brook which Bob might or might not have been able to negotiate came in view, and then, fortunately or unfortunately, there was a check.

Violet, pulling up, espied Hubert close behind her, and said, not without surprise, 'Oh, you managed to get over that place, then! How did you do it?'

'Flew the whole blessed thing,' answered the young man composedly. '*I* didn't know what was coming; only I supposed that, if you could do it, I could, and this worthy old beast of mine flung himself at it like a trump. You ought to have heard him grunt when he landed! It was a bit more than he had bargained for, I expect; but he had allowed himself just margin enough, and he's as proud as Punch now, I can tell you.'

'You mustn't try that kind of game in these parts,' answered Violet gravely; 'it won't do. We are not in Leicestershire, remember, and if you think that horse of yours can fly everything, you are very much mistaken. The chances are that a quarter of an hour later he would have killed himself and you too.'

'Oh, I expect we should take a lot of killing,' returned Hubert, with a laugh; 'we're neither of us worth very much, you see. Besides, we shall have time to get back our wind now. Have we lost that fox, do you suppose?'

Violet shook her head and replied that she was afraid so. 'This huntsman is a duffer,' she added in a lowered voice; 'he ought to have taken them straight on, instead of trying back. Well, I don't much care. Bob isn't really fit to go yet, and I'd rather take him home after this little burst than overtire him. You may see some sport yet, if you think it worth while to stay with them.'

But Hubert was not particularly keen about sport that morning. As soon as it became clear that the first run of the day was over, and that Miss Stanton meant to go home,

he declared that he had had enough of it, and
that he would accompany her if he might.
To this proposal she had no excuse for refusing
her assent; so that presently he was jogging
down a lane by her side and glancing at her
furtively every now and again, while she
busied herself with the lash of her hunting-
crop. It would take them, as he calculated,
the best part of an hour and a half to reach
St. Albyn's, during which time he would surely
be able to ascertain from her something which
he very much wanted to know. He began by
remarking :

'That old chap Amherst has been down
here, I hear. You saw him, of course?'

'Sir Harvey Amherst was here the other
day and was kind enough to call upon us,'
answered Violet demurely. 'I don't know
why you should call him an old chap, because
he really isn't so very advanced in years.
After all, though, I daresay he would seem
old to a boy like you.'

'Oh, come, Miss Stanton; one isn't a boy
at my age. As for that antiquated dandy, he

might look rather younger if he didn't try to look young. And I believe, if the truth was known, you think him quite as great an ass as I do.'

Violet turned her eyes upon her companion and surveyed him with an air of mild surprise. 'Oh, you are under the impression that I think Sir Harvey a great ass?' said she. 'In reality I don't think anything of the sort; I think him a very nice old—— that is, a very nice sort of person. But I wonder who or what gave you that impression?'

All of a sudden Hubert summoned up his courage and committed himself to a bold stroke. 'Ida did,' answered he. 'I don't mean that she said you thought the man an ass— though he is an ass—but she told me you had refused to marry him, and that's the best piece of news I have heard for many a long day. I could have kissed her when she told me : in fact, between ourselves, I *would* have kissed her; only I wasn't quite sure that she would like it.'

'It was a great breach of confidence on her

part to speak to you at all upon the subject,' said Violet severely, 'and I am very sorry that I let her into what ought, in justice to Sir Harvey, to have been kept a secret. So much for making a friend of a woman! I suppose the whole county will be informed of this piece of news now.'

'Oh no; indeed there is no fear of that!' the young man protested with great eagerness. 'Please don't be angry with poor Ida; I am sure she would never have dreamt of breathing a word about it to any one but me. Of course she told me——'

He paused, while his companion gazed interrogatively at him. 'Why was it a matter of course that Mrs. Chaine should tell you, if one may ask?' she inquired.

'Because she is a good, kind creature,' answered Hubert desperately; 'because she knows that I love you, and that, though I haven't the ghost of a hope for myself, it's something gained to hear that you aren't really what you chose to make yourself out. If you won't marry old Amherst for the sake of his money-bags, you won't marry anybody else from that motive. So you see I have some right to call this a piece of good news.'

It was a relief to him to have made his confession, and a still greater relief to observe that Violet was neither surprised nor angered by it. She rode on silently for some little distance before she remarked: 'It isn't my fault, you know.'

'Oh no; it's only my misfortune,' answered the young man, with due sadness and humility; 'I thought you wouldn't mind my telling you that I loved you, and I'm glad you know; but I never flattered myself that you could care for me.'

'That is not quite what I meant,' returned Violet; 'I meant that I am not to blame because, if I marry at all, I must marry somebody who is tolerably well off. Supposing that one could pick and choose—but that, you see, is simply impossible; so there's no use in thinking about it.'

'But if it were possible,' said Hubert, bringing his horse close alongside of hers and

turning an anxious, wondering face upon her
—' if you *could* choose?'

' Oh, in that case,' answered Violet laughing,
' I might choose you as soon as another—why
not? Only, as that isn't the case, and never
will be the case, we needn't bother ourselves
with it.'

Now, without being particularly clever, or
possessing any unusual insight into the in-
tricacies of feminine character, one may,
provided that one is a straightforward and
moderately courageous young man, understand
how to take advantage of admissions which
one has not been intended to take advantage
of. How it came to pass that, a few seconds
later, Hubert's left hand was grasping Violet's
right, while he was assuring her that nothing
except a little time and a little patience was
required to secure their eternal felicity, that
audacious youth would have been puzzled to
explain in any coherent way : probably very
few of us, if called upon to do so, could give a
clear or convincing account of the most important events in our lives. But what was

beyond doubt was, that this strange and unexpected event had happened, and in the presence thereof it could hardly be expected of
a happy-go-lucky fellow like Hubert Chaine
that he should condescend to mere sordid
questions of detail. Violet, however, was
more prosaic and more sensible.

'It's all nonsense,' she said, with a smile
which was not very far removed from being
tearful. 'When I tell my mother of this, she
will only say what is perfectly true—that we
aren't rich enough to marry and that long
engagements never come to anything. I ought
not to have allowed you—however, it is too
late to say anything about that now, and after
all I don't think I object to your knowing.
This much I can promise you : I will never
marry any man but you. As for marrying
you upon an income which only just keeps you
out of debt as it is—why, that of course can't
be done ; and the chances are that by the time
your income is doubled you will have forgotten
the circumstance of my existence. I shall
console myself with hunting, that's all.'

It will be readily understood that Hubert,
being in an exultant and sanguine frame of
mind, made light of such dismal forebodings.
Numerous lucrative appointments were open
to a smart young officer; it was true that he
had not yet passed the staff college, but doubtless he could do the trick—all sorts of fellows
did—and even if the worst came to the worst,
they would not starve upon what he had in
addition to his pay. Just look at the pull a
cavalry officer had over other people in the
item of horses' keep, for example! Oh, they
would get on all right, and they would always
manage to have something to ride, though
they might be put to the inconvenience of
living in a rather small house. In short, at
the end of a prolonged dialogue, he had extorted
every concession that he desired from Violet,
who could not help being in some measure
infected by his hopefulness. To be sure, she
had practically conceded everything by admitting to herself and to him that she loved him:
in so doing she had, as was inevitable, resigned
the prerogatives which for a brief season are

exercised by her sex in favour of those which
more properly belong to his.

'Now, I'll tell you just what you shall do,'
said he, when they parted—for indeed he had
not been slow to assume his newly granted
authority — 'you shall tell your mother all
about it, and towards five o'clock I'll drop in
to tea and be forgiven. She is bound to forgive us, you know ; she can't help it. We're
going to be awfully reasonable ; we're going to
wait a bit and see whether something won't
turn up ; only we're going to be true to each
other, whatever happens. Besides, I don't
believe you are really a bit frightened of her.'

'Not so much of her as of hard facts,'
Violet answered. 'Well, come at five o'clock,
then, and I'll give you a final answer.   I
haven't given you a final answer yet, mind,
though you choose to speak as if I had.'

And in truth she was under the impression,
on reaching home and endeavouring to put
a little order into her reminiscences of the
bewildering incidents of the morning, that
she had not actually surrendered her liberty.

She had, it was true, acknowledged both to herself and to Hubert that she was no longer fancy-free, and never could be so again; but that was surely not the same thing as having committed herself to an impossible engagement—for it really was an impossible engagement. The more she thought of it the more she became convinced that this talk of waiting for something to turn up was sheer rubbish. Things don't turn up—or at least, when they do, they turn up in favour of those who could do very well without them. *Vae pauperibus!* the poor of this world may be rich in faith; but if they cherish that kind of faith which consists in imagining that because they deserve to be happy just as much as bankers and brewers do, Providence will make rough places smooth for them, they are likely to have a rude awakening. After all, *on se console.* Violet did not think that she would easily find consolation; but she thought it extremely probable that Hubert would.

Thus she was in no mood to do battle with her mother, whom she succinctly informed of

the folly of which she had been guilty, and
who at once melted into tears.   Tears, as most
men, and even perhaps a few women, know
full well, are a formidable weapon with which
to engage in that species of warfare which
Mrs. Stanton felt it a sacred duty to declare.
One may, if sustained by a sense of spotless
integrity, withstand being stormed at; but to
be wept at (especially when one is conscious of
being in the wrong) is another matter, and Mrs.
Stanton made ample use of her advantages.

'This is just what I have always dreaded,
and always hoped and prayed that I might
be mistaken in dreading,' she sobbed.   'Never
in my life have I urged you to marry for
money; on the contrary, I have often been
shocked and distressed by the way in which
you have spoken about marriage.   But all
along I have had doubts about your sincerity;
all along I have said to myself, "This affectation of hard-heartedness will only lead up
to some dreadful catastrophe!"   And now it
seems that my suspicions were but too well
founded!   I was sure there must be some-

thing of this kind when you refused poor
Sir Harvey Amherst — a man against whom
there wasn't a word to be said, and whom
you yourself had done everything you could
to encourage.'

'I am not attempting to excuse myself,'
Violet answered humbly. 'I ought to have
taken Sir Harvey, and I ought not to be
engaged to a cavalry subaltern who is quite
sure to be indigent to the end of his days.
It is all very lamentable; only, somehow or
other, there is no help for it.'

'There *is* help for it—there *must* be help
for it!' returned Mrs. Stanton, drying her
eyes and assuming an air of dictatorship
which would have been comical enough if
it had not been backed by circumstances.
'You have been very wilful, Violet, and you
have been far too much indulged; but, when
all is said, I am still your mother, and I do
not believe that you will be so undutiful
as to contract an engagement which I forbid
—yes, positively forbid! I will not see Mr.
Hubert Chaine; I will not allow him into

my house; I will not give him the faintest shadow of an excuse for pretending—— However, if he is a gentleman, as I presume that he is, he himself will see that he is bound in honour to release you.'

'I don't know so much about that,' replied Violet slowly; 'but I certainly think that I am bound in honour to release him. I won't form any engagement without your consent, and I suppose you are quite right to withhold your consent; I should do just the same if I were in your place. Only I may as well tell you, once for all, that unless I marry Hubert Chaine I shall never marry.'

To that declaration Mrs. Stanton attached about as much importance as people of advanced years commonly do attach to similar declarations on the part of their juniors. She was surprised and thankful to find her daughter so submissive; she refrained from giving utterance to reproaches which she would have been abundantly justified in uttering; she kissed Violet and said:

'I am sorry, my dear—very sorry indeed

— that things should have fallen out so
unhappily. I wish they could have been
ordered otherwise ; but of course they couldn't
have been, and there's an end of it.'

Was there an end of it ? Hubert Chaine,
keeping his tryst at the appointed hour, and
being intercepted in the street by a young
lady who had come out for the express
purpose of informing him that he was for-
bidden the house, was by no means of that
opinion. Nor, as may be supposed, would he
hear of accepting the release so generously
offered to him.

'It's just the other way on,' he explained,
at the conclusion of a somewhat protracted
interview; '*you* aren't bound — how could
I ask you to be?—but I most distinctly am.
And until you have promised to marry some
other fellow I shall be every bit as much
bound as if your mother had sanctioned our
engagement—that I'll swear !'

'Then,' answered Violet, between laughing
and crying, 'I'm afraid you will be bound
for a very long time.'

Thus it is that youth defeats mature age, and conscience is outwitted by sophistry, and the affairs of this world get so out of gear that it seems scarcely worth while to do anything save shrug one's shoulders and thank Heaven that one's own wild oats were sown and reaped such a long time ago.

CHAPTER XXXI

COLD COMFORT

THE best inhabitants of this poor, disordered little planet are not the wise ones, nor the experienced ones, nor those who are so clever that they can detect a knave at a glance, and, upon principle, start by suspecting all their neighbours of knavery.

The above profound reflection is not put forward by the reader's very humble servant as a novel one, but merely as some sort of excuse for Hubert Chaine, who really would not have been the good fellow that he was if he had not been such a goose. Hubert never suspected anybody of knavery without good reason; like the law of the land, he assumed every man to be innocent until he had been proved guilty; like bull-dogs and all other honest creatures, he placed implicit

faith in such persons as had not, to his knowledge, ever played him false. And so—being
in some natural perplexity as to the course
which it behoved him to adopt with reference
to the girl to whom he had plighted his troth
—what must he needs do but betake himself to Chaine Court to seek counsel of his
elder brother! He found that eminently
trustworthy personage strolling round the
garden, and narrated his tale to him without
needless verbiage and with a good deal of
unstudied eloquence.

'I haven't forgotten,' he added, by way
of an afterthought, ' that the last time I spoke
to you about Miss Stanton you told me you
yourself had some notion of asking her to
be your wife; but I don't believe you were
serious at the time, and of course, even
if you had been, you couldn't think of such
a thing now.'

'Of course not,' agreed Wilfrid drily.
'Nevertheless, my dear fellow, it appears to
me that you have made a most egregious
fool of yourself.'

He spoke with some sharpness; for in truth he had been not a little vexed by the intelligence imparted to him. He had ventured to believe that Violet would be quite ready and willing to accept a husband so eligible in all respects as himself; and now, lo and behold! it turned out that she had been insane enough to yield to a school-girlish fancy for a younger son. Such a slight upon his own superior attractions was scarcely pardonable, and the effect of it was to make him thoroughly determined that he would beat his impertinent rival out of the field. To be defeated by Sir Harvey Amherst would have been honourable and endurable, because Sir Harvey's great wealth naturally rendered him a powerful competitor; but to be defeated by a whipper-snapper like Hubert would be a little bit too ridiculous. He therefore proceeded to remark somewhat disdainfully that calf-love is a transient complaint; that its ravages, as its name implies, are confined to the male sex; that women are much more given to talking than to acting sentimentally; and that, upon the whole, the wisest method of dealing with obvious impossibilities is to cease thinking about them.

'I didn't come here to consult you about that,' said Hubert, to whom these observations were anything but agreeable; 'I don't care two straws whether you sneer at what you are pleased to call calf-love or not, and I don't admit that what you set down as an impossibility is impossible at all. It is for Violet to say that it is impossible for us to marry upon a small income—and she hasn't said so.'

'Oh, hasn't she? I imagined from what you told me that she had.'

'Not at all!—at least, I don't think so. She won't consider herself engaged to me, because her mother bars the engagement: that's right enough, you know.'

'Perfectly right, no doubt; and it's a civil and considerate way of telling you to go about your business. I suppose Miss Stanton doesn't want to hurt your feelings more than she can help.'

'Oh, that's bosh!' returned the younger brother impatiently; 'it's very evident to me that you're talking about matters you don't in the least understand.'

'It may be so. I am singularly simple for my age, and I have never pretended to an exhaustive knowledge of feminine peculiarities. To the best of my poor ability, I have given you sound advice; but perhaps, after all, it wasn't advice that you wanted.'

'Yes, it was; only of course there's no use in your saying the sort of thing that every Tom, Dick, or Harry would say: we all admit that poverty and long engagements are objectionable. But you do know a good deal about women and a good deal about the world, and what I want you to tell me is, whether I'm doing the straight thing. I believe it's pretty well understood between us that I'm bound, but that she isn't. Well, that sounds fair enough; only I shall be sure to meet her, you see—out hunting and in the town and all that—and what sort of terms ought I to meet her upon?'

'Oh, if that's what you ask me, I can only answer that a gentleman ought to avoid all possible occasions of causing embarrassment to a lady. It isn't very difficult to take off one's hat and then get out of the way. You are afraid she may suspect you of being a faithless swain? My dear boy, you needn't feel the slightest alarm on that score. I will take it upon myself to affirm that she will never doubt your fidelity until you give her good reason—which, to be sure, you may do before you are very much older. And even then she will forgive you; for she has far more common sense than you can boast of. Meanwhile, you have it in your power to make her uncomfortable; so there can't be any question but that your duty is to efface yourself.'

'H'm! I shan't get much help from you, I see,' observed Hubert gloomily. 'You take it for granted that the whole affair is at an end.'

'At the risk of affronting you, I must confess that I do. And while I am being offensive, I may as well add that you should never have allowed it to begin. A man who can't afford to marry has no right to propose—upon calm reflection, you'll acknowledge that much, I daresay. Happily your indiscretion is not likely to have the serious consequences that it might have had; for, unless I am greatly mistaken in Miss Stanton, she is hardly the girl to waste the best years of her life in crying for the moon.'

Hubert went away very sorrowful. His brother's remarks had displeased him; but at the same time he could not help admitting the justice of some of them and the plausibility of others. It was quite true, for instance, that he had had no right to propose; and although what he had been guilty of had not in reality been so much a proposal as a confession, the result had been pretty much the same. Then again, it was true that he ought not to compromise Violet in any way, and that it might be considered ungenerous and ungentlemanlike to take advantage of the chance meetings

which her mother would probably be unable
to prevent.   But what he hoped was not
true—and what he was terribly afraid was
true—was that assertion of Wilfrid's that
Miss Stanton was not the girl to waste time
in lamenting the inevitable. She had, indeed,
assured him in so many words that she
would never marry any one but him; still
such assurances have been given and forgotten many and many a time since the
world began.   Moreover, he felt that he
was not entitled to hold her to a promise
of that kind. So it was poor comfort that
he obtained out of this visit of his, and,
being in such a depressed and disheartened
frame of mind, he went straight back to
barracks, instead of looking up Ida and laying
his case before her, as he had originally
intended to do.

It was, perhaps, just as well for him
that he decided to relinquish that intention;
for, had he carried it into effect, he could
hardly have avoided a somewhat ludicrous
encounter with two other persons who, from

opposite points of the compass, were now making their way towards the White House. Wilfrid, after his brother had left him, had come to the conclusion that it would be advisable to say a few words to Ida. Whether they should be friendly or unfriendly words he had not quite made up his mind: that would have to depend upon the spirit in which she might receive him. But either by means of conciliation or intimidation, she must be made to drop a scheme which did not suit the views of the head of the family, and which she seemed to have been chiefly instrumental in encouraging. It would probably be easier to conciliate than to intimidate her; still the latter course might be found practicable, if one were driven to it.

Wilfrid, therefore, having reason to know that women can be frightened when there is nothing at all to be frightened at, fetched his hat and stick out of the house and strolled off in the direction of a dwelling which ought by all right and precedent to have formed part of his property, but which was for the present occupied by a lady who, not content with having defrauded him of his due, had been presumptuous enough to place spokes in his wheels. So it came about that, when he had almost reached his destination, he was brought face to face with Miss Violet Stanton, who had walked over from St. Albyn's for reasons of her own, and who did not look altogether enchanted at meeting him.

'Are you going to the White House?' she asked, after she had acknowledged his salutation and had agreed with him that it was a fine day for a walk. 'I was rather in hopes of finding Mrs. Chaine alone.'

'In that case,' replied Wilfrid politely, 'I will turn back, of course. You have something very important and confidential to say to Ida, I suppose?'

'Yes; I want her to show me the last number of the *Mode Illustrée*, which I believe she is rich enough to take in, and to help me with a wrinkle or two out of it. One can't talk about these things with a man in the room; so, unless you have some special reason for wishing to call upon Mrs. Chaine this evening, it would be truly charitable of you to go home.'

It may have been that Violet was looking unusually pretty, or it may have been that there was something provocative about her manner, or again it may have been that consciousness of rivalry always acts as a stimulant; but, whatever was the cause that stirred Wilfrid's somewhat sluggish heart, certain it is that he suddenly experienced a longing to win Miss Stanton for his own which far exceeded in intensity any previous desire that he had felt to be so fortunate. Indeed, some symptom of this was recognisable in his voice, as he said:

'Your wishes are quite literally my law. I'll make myself scarce, since you want to be rid of me; though, if I were to consult my own inclinations, I should accompany you, notwithstanding the dressmaker. Happy will be the man who will eventually have the privilege of paying your dressmaker's bills!'

'Do you think so?' returned Violet, with

a quick, sidelong glance at him. 'Well, if such a man exists, or ever comes into existence, I daresay he will be rather happy, because I don't spend much on dressmakers. It is the tailors and saddlers who make havoc of my poor little allowance.'

'Ah, but he will have to pay them too, won't he? Lucky fellow, all the same!— that is, if he *can* pay. And you won't be so short-sighted as to link your fortunes with those of any man who can't, I trust. No, Miss Stanton, you know better than to fall into such a fatal error as that.'

He looked at her with a meaning smile, which she perfectly understood.

'I wonder who has told him?' she thought to herself. But she did not blush, nor was she much offended by his rather blunt fashion of depreciating his brother and recommending himself. She had not Ida's instinctive dislike for Wilfrid, who seemed to her to be a man of the ordinary selfish type, and who, had she been heart-whole, might have struck a bargain with her as easily as Sir Harvey Amherst.

'As far as I can see, there is every prospect of my paying my own tradespeople to the end of my days,' said she. 'Well, since you insist upon taking a broad hint, the least I can do in common gratitude is to let you go at once. I am sure Mrs. Chaine will be delighted to see you to-morrow or next day. Good evening.'

He was not anxious to be dismissed, because he had one or two more appropriate observations to make, and because (for in truth he did not very well understand a sex which he heartily despised) he fancied that the girl was not unwilling to listen to him; but she turned and moved away so abruptly that he was left without excuse for pursuing her, and she accomplished the short remainder of her walk unmolested.

Unfortunately, somebody is almost always in the way—perhaps even I who write and you who read are occasionally in the way, despite the quick-sightedness and discretion upon which we so justly pride ourselves—and Violet had much ado to conceal her

disgust when she found that long-legged
Arthur Mayne seated in her friend's drawing-
room. Arthur Mayne, for his part, having
that honesty and inability to disguise his
emotions which belongs to our masculine
nature, looked quite frankly disgusted at the
entrance of the visitor. 'Confound that girl!'
was the uncivil ejaculation which he inwardly
permitted to himself; 'she'll sit me out this
time, I suppose.'

This, however, was really an unwarrantable
assumption. Violet would have liked very
much to sit him out; but she soon perceived,
by Ida's slightly heightened colour and extreme cordiality, that that was not exactly
what her friend wished her to do; so she
chattered commonplaces for ten minutes,
hastily swallowed a cup of tea, and then
jumped up, without so much as having
asked for a glimpse at the *Mode Illustrée.*
Ida followed her out to the front door,
divining perhaps that she had come upon
some special errand, and said apologetically :

'I am so sorry I wasn't alone. Have you anything to do to-morrow afternoon?'

'Oh, if I don't turn up to-morrow, I will the next day,' answered Violet laughing. 'After all, I hadn't such a very extraordinary piece of news to give you—only that I have made an abject fool of myself. Would you believe that I, of all people, should have fallen in love with a hopelessly impoverished youth like Hubert Chaine, and, what's more, that I should actually have been and gone and told him so? But that is the lamentable truth.'

The embracings and congratulations which greeted this announcement may be easily imagined; but Violet soon extricated herself from both. 'We can't talk here,' she said; 'if you have anything to say to me which can possibly resist the attacks of reason and common sense, you will have to say it when we have time for ample discussion. You must go back to Mr. Mayne now and forget all about me and my sordid embarrassments.'

It must be confessed that Ida obeyed the above injunction to the letter. She did not

forget her friend's interesting difficulties when
she re-entered the drawing-room—indeed, her
mind was full of them—but she forgot them
soon afterwards, for the very cogent reason
that she was promptly called upon to face
difficulties of her own which interested her
still more. How many of us love our neighbours as ourselves? Certainly not Ida Chaine,
who, though a truly unselfish woman, was
quite unable to devote any part of her thoughts
to others from the moment that Arthur Mayne
embarked upon a statement which he had
come to her house for the express purpose of
making.

'The end of my holiday is coming into
sight,' he began; 'I shall have to go back
to work and London soon, and I can't go
without saying something to you which I
should have said before this if I hadn't felt
that it would most likely be useless. Useless
or not, it must be said. As far as that goes,
I suppose you know it already, Ida; I
suppose you don't require to be told that I
haven't changed, and that I love you just as

much as I did in the days when — well, to
speak honestly, when I believe that you loved
me. I quite understand that *you* must have
changed ; you couldn't have helped changing
in some ways ; but—can't we agree to sponge
out the past and everything that belongs to
it ? After all, it is dead and buried now.'

Ida shook her head. ' It is never possible
to undo what has been done,' she answered,
with tears in her eyes ; 'if one could only
realise that in time, what a difference it
would make and how many times we should
look before leaping ! We realise it clearly
enough when the leap has been taken, though ;
and nothing can ever make me what I used to
be. I should have thought you would have
understood that.'

' To me you are just what you used to
be,' returned Arthur ; and if this was not
strictly true, he believed that it was. ' You
haven't ceased to be yourself—else I should
have ceased to love you. Has it ceased to be
possible that you should love me ? Because
that is the only real question between us.'

'Ah no; that isn't the only question. You will see that it isn't if you will think for a moment of who I am and where I am now Of course it is possible—and a great deal more than possible—for any woman to love you.'

'You mean that you have become rich upon John Chaine's money,' said Arthur quickly. 'Yes; I know that, and I admit that it would be an obstacle if you chose to make it one. But I am perfectly certain that you would resign this wealth as gladly and willingly as I would for the sake of any one whom you cared for; and in reality it ought to be much more of an obstacle to me than to you. I have never thought so meanly of you as to consider it, and I needn't tell you that I would infinitely rather be without it. I have an income of my own to offer you now, and my prospects are as good as they can be. For a few years we might not be precisely well off, but we certainly shouldn't be in want.'

Ida made a gesture of dissent. 'It wasn't about that that I was thinking,' said she. 'If I were to marry again, this house would revert

to Wilfrid ; and as for the money that old Mr.
Chaine left me, I don't know that I should
feel any. scruple about keeping it, though I
should be quite ready to give it up. What
you don't choose to remember, and what other
people will never forget, is that I am the
widow of a murderer — at any rate, of one
who is supposed to have committed murder,
and who is supposed to have done so in consequence of the way in which I treated him.
However innocent I may have been, I must
bear the weight of that reproach to my dying
day—and I must bear it alone.'

She spoke sincerely ; she was determined
that Arthur should not suffer from any stigma
which might be assumed to attach to her ; she
was determined also that she would say nothing
about Barton's half-revelation until she should
have heard something more definite from the
man. But perhaps she may have hoped that
she would be urged to explain that hinted
doubt of hers as to her late husband's guilt of
the crime imputed to him. Arthur Mayne,
however, disappointed her by taking no heed

of an observation which seemed to him irrelevant.   Personally, it was a matter of in-
difference to him whether John Chaine had
committed one murder or twenty ; he only
asked to be allowed to forget John Chaine,
and he only cared to know whether John
Chaine's widow had similar inclinations.

'It all comes to this,' said he, after he
had vehemently protested against the absurd
notion that misfortune is synonymous with
disgrace : 'can you love me, or can't you ?
If you can, nothing ought to keep us apart : if
you can't, all you have to do is to say so ; and
then I will go away and trouble you no
more.'

Being thus driven into a corner, what could
Ida do but make what practically amounted to
an admission of the truth ?   Straightforward
people generally do manage to get at the truth,
and although Arthur Mayne neither heard it
in its entirety nor was permitted to hope that
Ida's conscience would ever let her marry him
under existing circumstances, he went away
full of joy and of confidence in the future.

That her future could be made to depend in
any way upon the clearing of her late husband's memory was too preposterous an idea to
be seriously entertained, and he wasted little
thought upon it. He knew now (notwithstanding her refusal to confess as much in
plain language) that Ida loved him : nothing
else really mattered.

Meanwhile, Ida, sitting alone in her drawing-room, with her hands clasped idly in her
lap and a glow of happiness in her dreamy
eyes, was saying to herself : ' If only that man
Barton was not deceiving me !—and if only I
can force him to speak out ! Arthur won't
see that it makes any difference ; but it does
make a difference—it makes all the difference!
And he would find it out sooner or later ;
because some woman out of the many who
would malign me would be sure to get to
his ear.'

Then she started up suddenly. ' I must
go and see Barton,' she exclaimed aloud ; ' I
can't bear this suspense any longer !'

CHAPTER XXXII

BARTON SPEAKS

I⊤ was still daylight, though the evenings were now growing short, when Ida set out to walk across the fields to the gamekeeper's cottage. She had received no direct news of him since her last visit, nor had she seen the doctor, to whom she had intended, in case an occasion should present itself, to speak a word or two about the man's physical and mental condition; but she had heard through the servants that he was a shade better, and it seemed likely enough that his life might be prolonged for a few more months. Now she felt that it would be utterly impossible to wait months for an elucidation of the mystery which he had partially revealed : moreover, she was persuaded that it would be quite wrong to do so. The very least that one can do for an innocent man who has died under suspicion of guilt is to establish his innocence the moment that any chance of establishing it arises; it is positively wicked to allow any such chance to slip, and unless Barton could be induced to disburden his conscience now, he might not improbably die without disburdening it at all. Consequently, she was not only able to acquit herself of any selfish motive in taking prompt action, but reproached herself for having been remiss inasmuch as she had not taken action earlier.

Philosophical dissectors of our composite nature have repeatedly sought to prove that our motives are at all times, and must necessarily be, selfish. Possibly their diagnosis may be correct; but at least we have the satisfaction of knowing that they will never succeed in making us believe anything of the sort, and as far as that question went Ida's mind was at ease while she passed with quick steps over the meadows, where the heavy autumn dew was falling and the melancholy stillness of the coming night was casting its

shadow before it. She had not loved John
Chaine; she had not pretended to love him,
nor had his treatment of her been such as to
earn her love; but she bore his name, she had
inherited what would have been his fortune,
her honour was in some sort involved in his,
and she was bound to neglect no opportunity
of setting him right with a world which, as
it appeared, had misjudged him. That was
enough: why trouble about secondary causes
when primary ones are all-sufficient?

And in fact she had not time to trouble
herself much about causes, being preoccupied
with the more practical problem of how to
open the lips of a man who obstinately prefers
to keep them closed. Barton was very obstinate; he was not—or at all events he did not
suppose himself to be—dying, and he evidently did not care enough about abstract
justice to run the risk of getting into difficulties for the sake of it.

'I shall have to frighten him,' thought Ida.
'After all, he must see that he has put himself in my power by confessing that he knows

who committed the murder, and if I threaten
to apply to the magistrates, he will probably
become more communicative.'

Whether this plan would have proved successful seems open to doubt ; but Ida was not
called upon to make trial of it ; for as soon as
she reached her destination she was accosted
by Mrs. Barton, who was standing at the
garden-gate, shading her eyes with her hand,
and who exclaimed :

'Lor', m'm, you *have* walked fast ! I
didn't think as you could ha' got my message
by this time.'

'I have had no message,' answered Ida ;
' did you send for me ? '

'Why, yes, m'm ; the gal started off run-
nin' to fetch you nigh upon an hour ago ; but
maybe she's stopped to pick blackberries—
children is so thoughtless ! '

'Is your husband worse then ? ' Ida asked
quickly.

The woman shook her head and raised the
corner of her apron to her eyes, though this
action seemed to be rather a conventional

tribute than the result of any immediate necessity. 'He's sinkin' fast, m'm,' she re-replied; 'I don't b'lieve but what it'll be all over afore this time to-morrow. Well, Barton he's been a 'ard man, and he's give me a 'ard life of it; but, put it how you will, it do come terrible upsettin' to be left alone like this, with a passel o' children to keep and nothin' for it but to take in washin'.'

Ida said as much in the way of condolence as her impatience would allow her to say, and then suggested that, if the sick man wished to speak to her, he should be enabled to do so forthwith.

'Yes, m'm,' answered the woman, eyeing her rather suspiciously; 'I'm sure I don't want to stand betwixt you, nor yet I don't know, no more than the babe unborn, what 'tis that he has to tell you. He's that close *I* can't get nothin' out of him, though when he was light-headed he let drop here a word and there a word, as one may say. But if he done wrong, you wouldn't go for to visit it upon the widow and the fatherless in their affliction, would you, m'm?'

Apparently Mrs. Barton was not less selfish than her betters. For the rest, she was a miserable-looking woman, who might very likely have led a miserable existence, and her misgivings were pardonable. Ida said what could be said towards reassuring her. 'If your husband has concealed anything which it was his duty to reveal, of course the wrong will have to be set right,' she remarked; 'but I don't suppose that will lay you or your children open to blame or loss. Will you take me to him now, please?'

Barton was sitting up in bed, supported by pillows and cushions; his breathing was laboured and irregular; his cheeks had the ghastly pallor of approaching death, and his great, gaunt hands kept plucking at the patchwork quilt which covered his knees. His eyes, however, when he opened them on Ida's entrance, had not yet lost their fire or vitality.

'You're none too soon, Mrs. Chaine,' said he hoarsely; ''tis all over with me now, and the sooner I'm gone the better 'twill be for

me.   Now, 'Liza, you get out of this and don't
come nigh me again till I send for you—d'ye
hear ?'

Mrs. Barton fetched up a tremendous sigh,
by way of protest, but retired submissively,
while Ida drew nearer to the bedside.

'Now, m'm,' began Barton, 'will you
please be so good as walk on the tips of your
toes to the door and see whether that woman
ain't got her ear to the keyhole? Ah, I
thought as much!' he added, when Ida had
obeyed his injunction, and when a sudden
scuffle of retreating slipshod feet made itself
heard. 'There's a stick in the corner by the
fireplace ; but maybe you wouldn't care for to
use it.   Well, I dessay she won't ventur' back
—not for a minute or two—and what I got
to say is soon said.   Look 'ee here, m'm,' he
continued, beckoning to Ida to approach, and
lowering his voice : 'I told you a while ago as
I knowd Mr. John were innocent o' that there
murder.   "Well," says you, as was on'y
nateral, "if he didn't do it, who did ?"
"Ah," says I, "I has my reasons for keepin'

o' that dark." Good reasons, too; though they don't amount to nothin' now. I'm agoin' to my account—so parson tells me—and "Repentance," says he, "can't never come too late." Not as I more 'n half believe un; 'tis what he's bound to say, d'you see; but 'tain't sense nor yet reason.'

'It *is* sense and reason,' returned Ida, in an agony of impatience; 'surely you can understand that if you die without doing justice to an innocent man whose innocence it is in your power to prove, the last act of your life will be a deliberate sin! What other sins you may have committed I don't know; but you can't hope that they will be forgiven unless you try to make some sort of atonement for all the misery that your silence has caused.'

' 'Twas 'ard on pore Mr. John, I'll allow,' agreed the man; 'but I can't make no atonement to he, nor I didn't accuse him neither; and as for others, I don't know so much about *their* misery. Well, least said soonest mended. 'Twas me as done that there job, m'm.'

Ida recoiled, half in horror, half in relief.

'You killed your master!' she ejaculated—
for, somehow or other, she had never imagined
that Barton could be himself the murderer.
'What for?—what had he ever done to you?'

'Give me the sack, that's all,' returned the
man sullenly; 'turned me adrift to beg my
bread. And what had I ever done to he?—
that's what I want to know. Perkisits there
may ha' been—I don't say to the contrary—
but I worn't the on'y one as claimed perkisits;
and to call a man a thief and put him out of
house and home for a thing like that!—well,
Mr. Leonard Fraser he worn't no gentleman,
that's the long and the short of it. Friend o'
yourn, I b'lieve, m'm, and played the fiddle as
well as most, I make no doubt; but he worn't
no gentleman.'

'Was that a reason for taking his life?'

'Maybe not; but if a man puts a pistol to
my head, I've a right to kill him, and that's
what Mr. Fraser done to me. Starvation—
't wasn't nothin' less than that as he threatened me with. So, thinks I to myself, there's
more lives depends on mine nor what there

does on yourn, and I makes up my mind to do for un. I knowd where he was goin' that evenin', I knowd which way he was bound to come back, and I waited for un and choked the life out of un easy enough. He was a pore, weakly critter, to be sure! Well, things fell out uncommon fortunate for me. 'T wasn't likely as I should be suspected, seein' as nobody but Mr. Fraser himself knowd how he'd served me; but 't was a bit o' luck as he should ha' had that tussle with Mr. John afore. Seemed a'most providential, as parson 'd say.'

Ida might have been more shocked by Barton's callousness if she had been less desperately eager to obtain some proof of the truth of his statement and less sensible of the danger of losing time. 'You will have to put this in writing,' said she; 'nobody will believe the story if you don't.'

'I've thought o' that, m'm,' the man replied; 'you'll find the paper under the piller there, with the signatur' duly witnessed by the doctor and the parson—which I told 'em 't was my will, and they didn't see nowt else but me signin' o' my name.'

And when Ida had possessed herself of the precious document, and had hastily run her eye over it, he implored her not to divulge its contents to any one until he should have breathed his last. 'I don't know but what they might drag me out o' my bed and string me up even now, d'ye see, m'm,' he whispered.

To a man in his state it seemed safe to grant that concession, and Ida did not refuse it. She begged him to confess all to the Vicar, whom she offered to go and fetch; but this he would not hear of, declaring that it would give him no comfort to do so, that he did not 'hold with' the doctrine of priestly absolution in any shape or form, and that he now only wished to be left to die in peace. He added: 'I ain't injured nobody as I knows on, without 't was the man as wanted to do me a injury; for 't wasn't me as got Mr. John into trouble. If there's one as did ought to make a clean breast of it to parson, I should say 't was Mr. Wilfrid.'

In this latter expression of opinion Ida was quite disposed to concur. Finding that she could do nothing with the half-repentant sinner, and being at length pointedly requested by him to go away, she left him and returned home, where she spent the best part of the night in pondering over his written statement and its probable consequences.

Before she had finished dressing the next morning a messenger came to tell her that Barton was dead.

END OF VOL. II

G. C. & Co.

Printed by R. & R. CLARK, *Edinburgh.*